ALIEN ORPHAN

FATED MATES OF THE SEA SAND WARLORDS
BOOK THREE

URSA DAX

NOTICES

This is a work of fiction. All characters, events, and incidents in this novel are fictitious and not to be construed as reality or fact.

Alien Orphan Original Copyright © 2021 Peace Weaver Press Inc. President Veronica Doran

Alien Orphan Alternate Print Cover Edition © 2023 Peace Weaver Press Inc. President Veronica Doran

Cover Design: The Book Brander Boutique

Alien Orphan Alternate Print Cover ISBN: 978-1-7381129-1-3

✤ Created with Vellum

ACKNOWLEDGMENTS

My process has not changed substantially from my last two books, nor have my acknowledgements. Like always, I want to sincerely thank my mother SMD and my husband RSH for their unwavering support no matter how weird my writing gets. Neither of them have blinked an eye at my strange little alien love stories and I couldn't be more grateful for my support system. I also want to once again thank all my dear readers, fans, and new friends that I have found along this journey. I never imagined I would connect with so many of you, or that so many people would enjoy my work. I am grateful for each and every one of you! Special thanks to The Book Brander for the special edition paperback cover!

AUTHOR'S NOTE

To this day, Melanie and Taliok's story remains a reader favourite in the Sea Sand series, and is one of my favourites, too. With this book, I felt I was really beginning to hit my stride as a scifi romance author and to step into my voice.

One of my favourite parts of writing is creating the characters, and Melanie and Taliok are two I will never forget. I don't think I'll ever stop loving our scarred, adoring Taliok and the way he so quietly and ardently supports our reserved heroine Melanie. There's something touching about how these two characters, each hurting in their own way, come together and heal each other in the end, and I couldn't be happier to give them a beautiful new special cover worthy of their love story.

-Ursa

1

MELANIE

"Well, this is something I never thought I'd cross off my bucket list," I whispered. I never thought I'd end up on an alien planet, let alone as a guest at a human-alien wedding. Although, the people of the Sea Sands didn't call it a wedding, they called it a Gahnala-Kai. A ceremony to mark the joining of a Gahn to his mate, and the naming her the Gahnala, queen of her tribe.

Kat snorted beside me at my words, muttering back, "You're telling me."

Despite the alienness of the whole situation, it was kind of beautiful in its own way. The evening fire had died down behind us, and we were facing the stark stone wall of the Cliffs of Uruzai, the dim firelight flickering across the jagged surface. Chapman and Gahn Fallo stood silhouetted against the rock, which was normally a deep copper colour, but was now black under the night sky. Above us, the ring of asteroids we'd once glimpsed from a space ship none of us had wanted to be on, shone in a line like pearls caught on a string. There were no cities on this planet, no lights besides the glimmers of the tribal fires, and the spray of stars above the cliffs was breathtaking, a million sharp teeth of light.

"Now the Gahn will offer his weapon to his Gahnala as a show of respect. To show that if she would kill him, he would let her," Bokeelie, one of the tribe healers, whispered to us.

"Dude, what?!" Kat hissed back. "Has anyone ever actually done that?"

"Of course not," Bokeelie said, the glimmering parts of her eyes tightening up as she looked at Kat. "No woman of the Sea Sands would ever kill her Gahn, let alone her own mate."

"What if he deserved it?" I asked, my voice flat, unable to help myself, but Bokeelie did not answer. Her words rattled around in my head. It was strange understanding the aliens' speech, now. Strange, but kind of nice, after all the chaos and confusion of our arrival. We'd been settling into our new home against the Cliffs or Uruzai for the human equivalent of a week after leaving Gahn Fallo's territory in the hills. The first thing we'd done when we'd arrived was get marched into the Lavrika's caves in the cliffs by Cece. Then we'd dunked into the milky pools there, one human after another, like some alien game of bob for the apples. Only this time it was bob for the magic Cupid dragon who will teach you how to talk. My memories of being in the milky pool were hazy. Some women claimed they'd seen something in the bright white – a huge creature with rows and rows of teeth. I hadn't seen anything, not even my own two hands in front of my face. But I'd felt something. The strong winding and squeezing of a serpentine body around mine. And luckily, it worked. All of us humans could now communicate with the people of the Sea Sands.

I turned my attention back to the ceremony in front of us. As Bokeelie had pointed out, Gahn Fallo had taken one of his many blades from his back and offered it, bone hilt-first, to

Chapman. While most of the alien men had a few weapons strapped to them at all times, along with the spears they often carried, Gahn Fallo's back was barely visible beneath his many, many blades. To be honest, it kind of seemed like overkill. But then again, almost everything about Gahn Fallo seemed like overkill.

Gahn Fallo's over-the-top-ness was balanced out by his new human mate. Chapman was tough, practical, and no-nonsense. "She'll be good for him," I said, mostly to myself, but I felt Kat glance over at me.

"Personally, I still think she's fucking nuts. Her *and* Cece."

Kat's eyes darted over to the other couple in question, Cece and Buroudei. Most of our human group was currently standing with Gahn Fallo's tribe on the sand. Cece was the only one standing with the other tribe, slightly set apart from us. But it made sense since she was now Gahn Buroudei's mate, and she'd been with his tribe from the beginning. She'd had her own Gahnala-Kai in Gahn Buroudei's territory before we'd all met up here.

This was the first time since we'd arrived that both the tribes had gotten so close to each other, and there was definitely some tension in the air. But no one had tried to rip anyone else's head off, yet. *So far, so good.*

Kat was looking ahead again, shaking her head incredulously as Chapman swung Gahn Fallo's black sword back and forth, as if testing the weapon's weight. Kat's sentiments were shared by a lot of the women here. Some of them could not understand feeling attracted to someone outside of your own species. Personally, I didn't find it all that weird. The aliens had some very odd features, including cropped Doberman-like ears and Kangaroo-like feet and tails, long black claws, and not to mention the fact that the shortest man among them was close to seven feet tall. But at the same time, the longer we spent with them, the more human they became. Not that being human was necessarily a good thing, though. Humans could turn on you at any moment, even the people you thought you knew best. The ones who claimed to love you. So, no, I didn't find the romantic interactions between human-girl and Kangaroo-dude weird. What I found unbelievable was how easily they trusted these new men. I could get attraction and lust. But deep, abiding trust? True love? With men you hardly knew? Yeah, that was something I was not on board with. Keeping your guard up at all times was the only way to stay truly safe. So far the people of the Sea Sands had been good to us, and I was grateful. It could have been a lot worse. But experience had taught me that it might not last. In fact, it probably wouldn't.

But I kept my gloomy thoughts to myself. Cece was beaming next to her mate across the sand from us, and Chapman was smiling more than I'd ever seen her smile before.

"This is the part where the Gahnala is supposed to give the weapon back," Bokeelie whispered, but a note of uncertainty laced her voice. Chapman was hefting the blade in her hand, her human fingers so small around its hilt that it looked totally absurd. Gahn Fallo growled something I couldn't hear, and Chapman's grin grew wider, almost devilish. Gahn Fallo's tail whipped behind him, and finally he seemed to get tired of Chapman's shenanigans. His huge hand shot forward, so fast it was like a fucking bullet, and he grabbed the sharp part of blade. Chapman swore and immediately let go, and a gasp went through the human women. I tensed, watching Gahn Fallo sheath his blade with a now profusely bleeding hand. Chapman's words carried over the sands toward us.

"*Jesus*, Fallo, you just got that arm working again! I could have taken your *damn* hand off!"

The swear words came out in English, a funny quirk of

4

our language acquisition that I had seen madden the two Gahns to no end as they tried to understand everything their mates said.

"You never would have taken my whole hand, my fiery one. A finger, perhaps," Gahn Fallo replied, sounding haughty. Chapman opened her mouth, about to shoot back some retort, when Gahn Fallo stepped up to her, brushing the knuckles of his injured hand across her cheekbone, streaking her freckled skin with his black blood. His next words were so quiet I barely heard them. "A hand, a finger, my whole body – it does not matter. It is all yours, to do with what you will." He growled then, taking his hand away. "My blade, however, is not."

I could see the giant roll of Chapman's eyes from where I stood. Kat snickered, and Bokeelie's tail twitched nervously.

"Your kind is very... bold," she said, frowning. Bokeelie's small son was nestled under her arm, his head leaning against her hip. Her mate, Vakal, was standing near Gahn Fallo. As his right hand man, he was almost always nearby his Gahn.

I couldn't help but agree with Bokeelie. It didn't exactly seem smart to antagonize the aliens any more than necessary, especially when they had that many knives and were certifiably insane (at least in Gahn Fallo's case). But not everyone was as cautious as me, and antagonizing kind of seemed to be Chapman and Gahn Fallo's whole vibe. There was nothing I could do but watch, and worry, and wait for the other shoe to drop.

Or, er, whatever the alien equivalent would be. None of these guys wore shoes on their long, three-toed feet. Or much clothing at all, besides loincloths and straps for their weapons. The women were a little more covered, wearing long tunics made of woven peet grass, often belted with a dakrival-hide strap at their waists.

From what I could see, Cece had jumped headfirst into the alien fashion. She was barefoot. Her chestnut hair fell in a long braid down her back, and she wore one of those same alien tunics, belted. Something I'd never seen her wear before, an elaborate arm-piece of woven grass and shimmering black beads, snaked up her arm. Bokeelie must have noticed me looking, because she leaned down towards me to explain.

"It is the Gahnala-Kai Rek. Normally a Gahnala wears it around her tail. It is only worn for special occasions. See, Kalla brings one for Chapman now."

Bokeelie pronounced Chapman the way all the aliens did – with a hard C sound, almost like Capman. I followed Bokeelie's gaze to see Kalla, the oldest woman of Gahn Fallo's tribe and one of the healers who'd helped us a lot, stepping forward and holding something delicately in her clawed hands. She handed it to Gahn Fallo, who in turn began to wind it around Chapman's bare arm. Unlike Cece, who was dressed in the style of the Sea Sands, Chapman wore the grey tank top and pants that we all did, the uniform from the ship. Though, since it was night time, none of us needed the solar protection jackets. She wore her red hair in the classic, neat, military-style bun she usually did, in contrast to Cece's braid. And her Gahnala-Kai Rek was different from Cece's, too. Evidently each piece had been created in the style of the tribe from which it came. Where Cece's was made of intricately braided peet grass fibres with hundreds of small, round black beads, Chapman's had longer, more roughly-cut, sharper-looking black beads, and the peet grass braiding was interspersed with the white and indigo petals of the rindla flowers from Gahn Fallo's hills. The beads on both pieces, though, seemed to be made from the same material as the shining black weapons the men carried. Back on Earth I'd been studying to be a geologist, and I was itching to get a closer look at whatever that material was.

"Aw, sweet, it's like an alien weddin' ring," Theresa said from somewhere behind me as Gahn Fallo finished lacing the long piece of jewellery around Chapman's arm, from wrist to shoulder. I could hear the smile in her voice, and I couldn't help but smile softly back. Theresa was so kind. So trusting and open, like a Southern ray of sunshine. Sometimes I wondered if it were better to be that way.

Better, maybe. But not safer.

But as Chapman grinned up at Gahn Fallo, and Gahn Fallo's bleeding hand lingered on her own, intertwining their totally mismatched fingers, I wondered if maybe Theresa had it right. Maybe this was good and safe and something to rely on. Maybe I really didn't have to worry anymore. Maybe, finally, things would be OK for me. For all of us...

But then the sound of war cries cut the air, throttling from across the open sands. The scene descended into chaos, the men drawing their weapons, while Bokeelie and the other alien women hustled us, along with their children, back to the tents. I clenched my jaw, keeping low while Kat stumbled and cursed beside me. I grabbed her arm to steady her.

"Less swearing, more running," I hissed at her, and she clamped her mouth shut, focusing on her feet.

We made it back to the largest tent, the human tent, that stood alone from all the others, nestled in a curved part of the cliff face. As I scurried through the tent flap along with the others, I turned my head just in time to see men on irkdu racing towards us from the open desert, weapons drawn.

And all those thoughts of trust and joy and safety went to fucking shit.

Theresa was wrong. And I was right. Unfortunately.

7

I didn't want to be right. I didn't want to live on edge, unable to trust, always waiting for something bad to happen.

But that was just how the alien cookie crumbled. Just like the cookies on earth. Crumbs everywhere. Making a goddamn mess.

Shit.

2

TALIOK

"There it is, Gahn!"

It took me a moment to realize that Oxriel was speaking to me as we thundered over the plains on our irxdu. The title of Gahn did not yet sit easily upon my shoulders, and I was beginning to suspect it never would. It was never a title I had sought, never one I'd asked for. And whenever I heard the word, I expected my predecessor, the mighty Gahn Irokai, to respond. But he was a dead man, now, slain by Gahn Fallo. And he had named me his successor.

Emptiness in the shape of him was stark around me as I grunted at Oxriel, looking at what he was pointing at. The long dark line of his bone and zeelk spur spear was aimed across the sand at a great dark structure. *So this is what Gahn Buroudei told me about. The dead flying thing that brought the new women to our desert.* He said they had come from another world, beyond Zapthrinax, beyond the sky and stars. It still seemed impossible. Unfathomable.

But then again, the new women, and my new mate, with all her wondrous, foreign beauty, was unfathomable, too.

"We are getting close," I said, bending lower over my hulking mount, urging it to go faster. The Cliffs of Uruzai were a dark line in the distance. It was to be our new home, with two of the other tribes of the Sea Sands and the new women. I never would have consented to such a thing before, I never would have obliged to live with the Gahns Fallo and Buroudei, but everything had changed with the arrival of the new women. And with my summoning to the pools of the Lavrika, where I'd glimpsed my mate's strange face.

My mate.

Like the title of Gahn, the thought of my mate, too, felt strange. But maybe it was because she *was* strange. I knew nothing of her, or her people. Not her name, not a single word of her language. I knew nothing of her voice, her mannerisms. I knew nothing of the body beneath her clothing, though that thought was a hot stab of pain mixed with desire.

I knew nothing of her, yes.

But I would learn.

And Gahn Irokai, if he were still living, would confirm to any man who asked that I had always been a diligent student.

The cliffs were expanding as we got closer. Soon, I would be with my mate. Soon, I would hold her in my arms and take her to my bed of hides. And finally, I would know joy again.

Since seeing her in the pools, and then again at the battle with Fallo's men, I had not been able to shake her from my mind. Her small round face, her white and brown eyes, and her long dark hair followed me everywhere, appearing behind my eyes before I slept, igniting my body and quickening my heart. I had barely registered the other women when I'd seen her in Gahn Fallo's hills. She'd shone like a star in my darkness, a great pulse of light that almost blinded me until I could see nothing else.

Well, I did know one thing about her.

When Buroudei's mate had been reunited with their group, the women had smiled widely, laughed, and been exuberant. My mate's lips had turned upward only briefly, before her face closed back down again.

It seemed my strange and painfully lovely mate did not smile much.

But it was no great matter.

Neither did I.

Soon, I would see her. I would touch her. And I would learn everything else there was to learn.

But first, I had to kill Gahn Fallo.

"Faster!" I commanded, and both my irkdu and my men obeyed. It was just a small party of us. Oxriel and three other warriors and me. I had ordered some unmated men to stay behind and guard our territory. The rest of our tribe's men were further back, moving much more slowly, accompanying the women, children, and elderly, bringing up the rear with our tents and other supplies. It had been a great task to prepare to move our people from our mountains to the Cliffs of Uruzai, and finally we were almost there.

The Cliffs of Uruzai were a truly impressive formation. Sprawling, cascading rock that went on for thousands of paces, carving the horizon. I had visited these cliffs only once, when the Lavrika had called me more than twenty-five days ago, but I knew that there was more to them than the Lavrika's caves. Those caves made up only a tiny portion of one small part of the cliffs. The rest contained peaks and valleys and ravines and clearings. Endless walls and gaps and tunnelling rock. It was almost as large and imposing a rock formation as the mountains of my people. Almost.

As we got closer, my sight stars pulled inwards. I scanned the rock face, searching for signs of the new settlements. The deal we'd struck was that the new women would live together in a central, neutral location, and that the other tribes would exist around them. But I had not yet seen with my own eyes how such a settlement had taken shape.

We passed the small, dark opening that was guarded by the Lavrikala. The opening to the caves where I'd seen my mate for the first time. Even as we sped past, I raised my tail over my eyes in respect for the guardian of the Lavrika. When I lowered it again, she was far, far behind us.

We raced along the edge of the cliffs, quite close to the rock, but I brandished my spear towards the sands.

"Back to the sands! We will have a better view."

Oxriel raised his own spear in return, crying out, and we peeled away from the rock, continuing along the cliffs but further out now. My breath pounded in and out of my chest. My fist was tight upon my spear. My eyes tracked back and forth, looking for any sign of life or movement.

Ah. There. Ahead. The embers of a dying fire.

My men had already seen it. We raced towards it, and the scene started to take shape. Two groups stood, slightly separated, facing two lone figures against the cliffs. I sucked in a breath and hissed as I realized that those two figures were Gahn Fallo and one of the new women. Gahn Fallo was winding a Gahnala-Kai Rek up the new woman's arm. I recognized the woman. It was the angry one with the fire hair who had challenged Gahn Buroudei in battle. *So the Lavrika has granted Fallo a mate from among the new women, too.* It was a shame she would have to watch him die the night she was named his Gahnala.

It would not have been my first choice to kill a man during his Gahnala-Kai. But Gahn Fallo deserved no courtesy and no such considerations. He'd killed my Gahn, Gahn Irokai, the man who'd raised me as a son. And thus he'd doomed himself to die by the bite of my blade.

I pulled that blade from my back now, raising it with my

free hand. This blade had belonged to Gahn Irokai, once. It felt heavy in my hand, but the longer I held it, the more right it felt. I slashed its huge, swooping scythe of a blade through the air.

I said nothing as we approached, but my men began shouting, their war cries echoing in the night. They knew I meant to kill Gahn Fallo. Their voices split the air, hungering for blood. My voice did not join theirs.

I never cried out in battle as some men did. My promise for vengeance against Gahn Fallo was a silent one.

But no less deadly.

The scene before us collapsed into madness as our presence was detected, women and children running, warriors drawing blades and gnashing fangs. I did not see my mate, nor did I look for her. I had to focus on my first task. I had to kill Gahn Fallo before I saw her, otherwise my mind would forever be torn from its duty.

We were close, now. I broke my silence.

"Remember my orders!" The words came quickly as we charged. "Remember that we are not here to wage war. We are outnumbered. I will kill Gahn Fallo, and that will be the only blood shed here tonight. Fight only if your lives are threatened."

I knew my men would not like such orders. It was not our way. Our ways were of the blade. But they would heed me.

"Yes, Gahn Taliok!" Oxriel cried. He and the others fell back slightly, lowering their weapons. I charged ahead, my irkdu forcing the crowd of warriors on the ground to part. Gahn Fallo's mate was gone, and he faced me alone, his long arms spread wide, each holding a large blade. I eyed those arms distastefully as I leapt from my mount, stalking towards him.

It was a pity Gahn Buroudei had not cut off Fallo's arm when he had the chance in battle.

Or his head.

But perhaps it was not such a pity, after all. Because now I would have the honour of avenging Gahn Irokai and wiping the stain of Gahn Fallo from the sands of our people.

Fallo stood waiting, his arms still spread wide. His fangs glistened under the light of the stars and moons as he grinned at me wildly. I did not return his dark expression of mirth.

"Have you come to taste my blade, Taliok, the way Gahn Irokai did?" His smile got wider. "Your old Gahn found it bitter."

Referring to Irokai as Gahn, but not me, was meant to be an insult. I ignored it. I did not let rage explode into shattered madness inside me the way Fallo did. My rage was cold and silent and drawn to a sharp black point.

Where Fallo was fire, I was stone.

And with that stone, I would crush him.

I hefted Gahn Irokai's blade, *my* blade, in one hand, my spear in the other. The warriors of Fallo's and Buroudei's tribes gathered in a loose circle around us, watching, waiting, tails snapping.

Fallo hissed and bent his legs, digging his feet into the sand, preparing to launch and strike. I did not give him such a chance. Weapons high, I vaulted forward.

I swung my huge, ablik scythe blade down just as Fallo's two blades came up to meet it, crossing over each other beneath mine. He grunted, and one of his arms faltered slightly when our blades connected with a crash. Blood poured from his flinching hand, though I did not think I had cut him yet. Taking advantage of whatever this momentary weakness of his was, I yanked my spear up, slicing at the underside of his faltering arm with the zeelk spur. He hissed at the contact, but pressed his two blades harder against mine, forcing them up, up, up, his feet scrabbling in the soft sand. Gahn Fallo was taller than me, one of the tallest warriors of the Sea Sands, but where I was shorter, I was wider, more heavily packed with thick muscle. With a snarl, I ripped downward with all my strength, forcing his weapons back down. The small victory fuelled me, dark heat in my veins, and I twirled my blade in my hand, pulling it back hard towards myself. The curved edge of my blade caught on one of Fallo's, the one in his weaker hand, and his weapon fell down to the sand, sliding towards me. I used my blade to hook it out of his reach, simultaneously raising my spear to block the thrust of his other arm. He was reaching for another blade from his back, now, but that could not stand. I would not let him get that far. He'd die before he ever touched it.

Chest heaving, I thrusted hard with my spear, knocking Fallo's arm away from me and stepping forward, swinging my long blade up as I did so. The blade heaved towards his throat, ready to end him...

The hard press of a blade bit beneath my jaw. I froze, wondering how Fallo had managed to get another weapon against my throat so quickly. But Fallo was standing still, one arm bleeding, empty-handed, at his side, the other still holding a blade half-raised against my spear. It was not him.

Gahn Buroudei's voice boomed from beside me

"Do not do this, Gahn Taliok. Do not kill him."

My rage doubled. It was no longer just directed at Fallo, but now Buroudei as well. How dare he keep me from my vengeance, something I had promised myself on the body of my dying Gahn? I had sworn it, sworn that I would kill him. My jaw locked hard as I stared at Fallo. My blade looked good against his neck. One flick of my wrist would bring that curved blade across his shoulders, rending his head from his body. But could I do it before Gahn Buroudei killed me?

Fallo glared at both of us, his sight stars spinning and

pulsing furiously. His broad chest heaved, his neck bunched with tense muscle against my blade. I could do it… I could do it, so quick, quicker than the beat of a brazelbird's heart…

I looked at Buroudei from the corner of my eye, not moving. I did not want to kill him Buroudei I could avoid it. He was not my friend, but he had allied with my Gahn Irokai against Gahn Fallo not long ago. Buroudei was a good sort of Gahn, honourable, though he was not of my tribe.

But then again, now he was allying himself with Gahn Fallo against me.

"Let me have this, Buroudei. Let me kill him. We will all be better off," I muttered, my words coming out as a deep growl.

My gaze moved back to Fallo, who was smiling now. It was a disconcerting combination – the smile of his wide mouth under the hatred in his eyes.

"I do not doubt it." Buroudei's words came heavy. "But Gahn Fallo killed Gahn Irokai in battle when *we* attacked his tribe. It was a fair kill, and he did not break from the ways of our people by doing such a thing. We all lost men in that battle, and we will lose many more if you commit this act now."

Fallo's tail thrashed behind him in the sand, and his smile turned into a snarl.

"You speak as if I would let him do it," Fallo hissed at Buroudei, his hand tightening on the blade he still held. Then, a high, hard voice rang out.

"And you speak as if *I* would let him do it."

My eyes flicked over to the sound, just for half a moment. *The red-haired woman. Fallo's mate.*

Like Buroudei's mate, it seemed this woman could speak with our words, though some of them were accented strangely, and some of them I did not recognize at all. Fallo wrenched his head towards her as she strode towards us. His movement sliced some of his skin against my blade. My body tensed as I watched the black wetness of it roll down to his shoulder. *Not enough. Not nearly enough.*

Fallo would have to give all his blood to the sands to make up for what he'd done.

Buroudei's blade pressed a little harder against me in return, and I clenched my fangs tightly as Fallo's mate reached us. She planted her feet in a wide stance next to her mate, placing her hands upon her hips in an odd posture I did not understand.

"Look, *bucko*, I don't know you yet. But I've already told both these boneheads that if you want the human women near you, there's no killing. None. *Nada. Zip.* You hear me?"

I stared at her for a long moment, not understanding. Finally, I ground out,

"What is she talking about, Gahn Buroudei?"

His tail swished.

"It is true," he said, "All of the new women, up until now, have been living with Gahn Fallo and his tribe. They feel allied to them, and they did not want to come here with us. They came only on the condition that there would be peace. If you kill Gahn Fallo now, you risk losing all access to them." His voice fell lower. "I know you have a mate among the new women. Do not let your need for vengeance separate you from the greatest joy this life has to offer before you even get to touch her skin."

A muscle in my cheek jumped. I did not move. If I moved, my whole body might split down the middle, torn apart by two equally ferocious desires. The desire to avenge Gahn Irokai. And the desire to claim my mate.

"'The greatest joy this life has to offer?' That's a new name for me I haven't heard yet. I like it."

Gahn Buroudei jerked at the sound, and my eyes flicked

away from Fallo and his new woman to see Buroudei's mate now marching towards us.

Is every one of new women going to come and interrupt my work?

There was only one new woman I'd welcome here, now. Only one I wanted. And she was nowhere to be seen.

The cold reality of what Buroudei had said sliced through me. If I killed Fallo now, then I might never see her again. *Don't lose her before you even get to touch her skin...*

I remained silent, thinking, as the red-haired women turned her attention to her mate under my blade.

"And you, what do you think you're doing! I told you, no fighting!"

Fallo drew a sharp breath, staring at her, as if no longer aware of me and my blade.

"I did not start this battle!" he cried, but his woman did not seem convinced. Her eyes rolled in a strange, almost stomach-turning way, the grey parts moving upward, showing the whites. I swallowed hard and looked away, my attention caught by Buroudei, now. He was holding up his free hand in the air, as if to keep his mate back.

"Zeezee, why have you come back here with Chapman? You should be at the tents, where it is safe!"

Zeezee flicked her braid over her shoulder and took a similar pose to Fallo's mate, Chapman.

"When I saw it was Gahn Taliok I figured it would be OK. For a second I thought it was some enemy I hadn't met yet coming to attack, but it's not." Buroudei's Gahnala fixed her gaze on me.

"Come on Taliok, we're friends, right?"

I grunted. We had been allies, once. Now, I was not so sure.

Her strange little face softened. I was not familiar with

these new women and their features and expressions, but I swore it almost looked like... Pity?

"Look, I know this is hard for you guys. This isn't your culture, this isn't your way. But Buroudei's telling the truth. Both Chapman and I have agreed that there can't be any violence among the three tribes represented here, or this will never work. And we're Gahnalas, now, and leaders of the human women, so you really need to listen to us."

I could feel my chance at vengeance slipping further and further away, like blood along a sharp blade. If I agreed to these terms, I would never get my chance to kill Fallo. But if I rejected them and killed Fallo, I might lose my own life, and certainly the chance to claim my mate. The past and the future reared up, two great fighting beasts inside me. The past, one ruled by war and battle and a deep love for Gahn Irokai, thundered against the future, a future bright with the face of a woman I did not yet know, but longed to.

The past was dark with blood. The future blinding.

And slowly, slowly, that light was winning out. Vengeance against Fallo would be sweet. But against the loss of my mate, it would become nothing but bitterness.

It took every bit of will I had to wrench my blade away from Fallo's neck, and I had to turn from his taunting grin in order not to bring that blade right back up. Half a moment later, Buroudei's blade fell away from my throat, and he pulled his Gahnala Zeezee against his side. The warriors who'd been watching our exchange around us began to relax, and I turned to my men.

"Dismount in peace and prepare for the arrival of the rest of the tribe."

Oxriel raised his tail, and the others followed, lowering themselves to the sand from their irkdu. Fallo's Gahnala dragged him away from the scene, her shoulders set fiercely.

The further away he got, the further away I felt from my vow of vengeance. It would not come to pass, now.

The hole left by Gahn Irokai felt a little larger, a little emptier, as I watched Fallo walk, still living, away from me.

I am sorry, my Gahn.

I was startled from my thoughts by a soft voice directly beside me. Jerking, I looked down to find the Gahnala Zeezee right next to me, staring up at my face.

As far as I knew these women were not hunters, but by the sands was she quiet! Unnervingly so.

"What did you say?"

In my jerking reaction, I'd missed the actual content of her words.

"I said thank you," she said with a smile. Gahn Buroudei hulked directly behind her, his eyes on my blade, which I finally sheathed at my back. In a final, painful show of peace, I tossed my spear to the ground.

"Thank you for not killing Gahn Fallo. I know you wanted to."

I grunted. *Wanted.* If she knew the depth of my desire in that regard, there was no way she would have stopped me. But I did not argue with her. It would do no good.

Her voice fell to a whisper.

"Taliok, will you tell me who your mate is?"

I stiffened. For some reason, I did not want to tell her. I wanted to keep my mate completely to myself, away from the prying eyes of others, even those of her people. But of course, that would be impossible. Now that we were going to be living so close to the other tribes, it would be found out, soon enough.

"I do not know her name," I admitted, clenching my fists. Involuntarily my gaze moved from Zeezee's face to scan the area around us, but all I saw were other warriors. The new women were evidently in hiding, away from the carnage I'd meant to inflict on Fallo. "She has dark hair, like our people, and eyes like yours. White and brown." When I'd first seen her in the pools, I'd thought those eyes were terrible. But now I wanted nothing more than to look at them once more.

"Hmm," Zeezee said, chewing her lip. "There's a couple of girls with dark hair and brown eyes."

"She does not smile much," I added, giving Zeezee the only other piece of information I had gleaned. Realization dawned on her face immediately.

"Oh, that must be Melanie. *Shoot.*" I did not recognize that last word, shoot, but I recognized the way Zeezee's face contracted. She seemed worried.

"What? What is it?" I growled, stepping towards her. Buroudei growled in return, drawing her into his chest. I ignored him. "What is wrong? Is she alright? Is she safe?"

"Oh, yes! Sorry, yes, nothing to worry about in that sense. I just..." She paused, her small forehead wrinkling before blowing out a breath. "I just think she might be one of the harder ones to convince about this whole... Mate thing."

A claw of worry wrapped around my heart.

"What do you mean, *convince?*" The Lavrika had spoken. It had awoken the sacred mate bond. There was nothing left to do but to live as mates from this day forward. No one had ignored the Lavrika's call in many generations.

"Well, some of the girls are more... open... to you guys than others. Melanie is pretty reserved and closed-off. You're going to have to really work to earn her trust, and get her to open up, I think."

I felt my brows contract in confusion. There were so many questions whirling in my head that I did not even know where to start. Gahn Buroudei, who had already lived through the confusion of claiming one of these strange women, spoke from above his mate's head.

"The sacred mate bond does not awaken in the new

21

women the way it does for us. They call it *falling in love*. And it is a maddening, inconsistent, and slow process."

Zeezee scowled, tilting her head back against his chest to look up at him.

"Slow? Pretty sure you didn't have to wait very long to get some of this human loving."

"It is slow on our terms. Men of the Sea Sands are not used to waiting for their mate's love." Buroudei muttered, bending down and speaking to her. Then he turned his face back to me. "Once a new woman falls in love, it is like the sacred mate bond. But it is not quick, nor is it guaranteed."

A cold wind swept through me, seizing in my blood. My fists shook, and I felt my face twisting. My mate felt no sacred mate bond for me? She did not feel as I did, that the entire world had shifted beneath her pretty feet? She had to *fall*, somehow, in order to be my mate? I could not imagine any scenario where she would fall, *could* fall, where I would not be there to catch her. Would such a thing not be dangerous?

"Don't look like that!" Zeezee gasped, seeing my face. I wondered what I must have looked like. Between my expression and my scars, it was probably a terrifying image. She kept speaking. "I said it might be hard, but not impossible. Look at Gahn Fallo, he somehow got Chapman to fall for him. If he can do it, you totally can."

Her words heartened me. She was right. Fallo had been successful with his mate. And everyone knew he was a mad fool. If such a fool could, as Zeezee said, make a new woman *fall in love*, then so could I.

"How does she fall? And where? I do not want her body to be hurt," I asked.

Zeezee groaned, then laughed, and Buroudei grinned. Their expressions did not put me at ease. I bit down a growl.

"What?" I grumbled.

"Oh, nothing," the Gahnala said. "Sometimes I just forget how many differences there are between us. Buroudei and I had a conversation like this in the beginning, too. But by that point, I was already too far gone. He didn't have to do much more to get me to fall for him. And it's not literally falling, by the way. It's a figure of human speech. It just means to awaken the sacred mate bond, basically. But you have to do it yourself. The Lavrika won't do it for you."

With a harsh sigh, I cast my eyes up to the sky, scanning the stars. Even the endless reach of the sky did not seem as monumental as the task before me. Awaken the sacred mate bond in my mate without the help of the Lavrika? Such a thing was unheard of. *It must be impossible.*

But Zeezee's words echoed in my head.

If Fallo did it, so can you.

Now that my vow for vengeance had been broken, I needed a new one. A promise that would drive the force of my life. I did not say it out loud, but it pounded through my body with a ferocity that drowned out everything else.

I would make my mate, my Melanie, fall in love. It would be done. *I* would do it.

If I could not kill Fallo, I swore I would do this instead. But as I stared up at the stars above, I worried that, between killing Fallo and winning my new mate, the latter would be harder. Much harder. I was a strong warrior, and now a Gahn, but for the first time in my life I looked at the task before me not with fierce and silent determination, but hesitation and doubt.

I was not used to such a feeling.

And I did not like it.

3

MELANIE

"Can you move over a bit, Kat? I can't see," I said.

Kat shifted, holding the flap of our tent open a little wider and crouching down so I could look out over her head.

"Why does it feel like we're always hanging out in the tent, watching the action unfold?" Kat muttered. There was a hint of bitterness in her voice, and I laughed humourlessly.

"You'd rather be out there with them?" I asked.

Them was Fallo, Buroudei, the other warriors, and the five new men who'd charged in on their irkdu. One of them had dismounted, and was approaching Gahn Fallo, weapons drawn. His spear looked like the others we'd seen, but his blade, a long, terrifying, scythe-like curve, was unique.

Kat looked up at me, her big blue eyes dark in the dim valok candlelight of the tent.

"Well, I'm not saying I want to be right in the middle of it," she replied. "But back home I never ran from a fight. Plus aren't you dying to know what's going on?"

I was curious, and I squinted, trying to get a sense of the scene. I wanted to know what was going on. I needed to know, because watching and observing and understanding the threats that may be coming your way was the only way to stay safe. I felt my face fall into blankness as my eyes scanned back and forth. The men were too far for us to hear their words, but Gahn Fallo seemed to be egging the new aggressor on. Classic.

"Personally, I just wish they'd stop all this fightin'," Theresa said with a sigh, plopping down onto a bed of hides behind us. Serena and a few others spoke words of agreement and went further into the tent. "Let us know if anythin' crazy happens. Otherwise, I'm gettin' some shuteye."

"You got it, Cap'n," Kat muttered, crowding closer to the tent's opening. Though Theresa and some others had given up on this fucked up spectator sport, there was still a group of about eight of us all trying to see out. Cece and Chapman hadn't even made it all the way inside the tent and were watching from just outside. Chapman stood still, hands on her hips, eyes narrowed, while Cece paced, worrying her nails between her teeth.

"Oh shit!"

Kat's exclamation wrenched my gaze from Chapman and Cece back towards the cliffs. Gahn Fallo and the new alien warrior were locked in combat, blades crashing. Gahn Fallo was taller than his opponent, but they seemed equally matched for strength, and it looked like the new guy was about to gain the upper hand. I clenched my jaw, my stomach plummeting. I obviously didn't love Gahn Fallo the way Chapman did, but I didn't want to watch him get killed tonight, either. That would throw things into chaos yet again. And so far, chaos was all we'd known here.

There was a flurry of movement, and some warriors got closer to the fight, blocking our view.

"Oh, come on," Kat groaned. I shared her frustration, and heat mounted in my neck, anxiety about not knowing what was happening. But then, Chapman made a sound, said "Goddamnit, Fallo," and started running, parting the warriors before her as they moved out of the new Gahnala's way. That break in the crowd allowed us to see that Gahn Buroudei had stepped in. His knife was at the new guy's throat, but the new guy also had his own huge curved blade against Gahn Fallo's neck. Two parts of a Mexican standoff. I breathed out slowly, forcing myself to take in every detail of the scene. *Don't miss anything. Pay attention.*

Chapman reached the scene, and there was definitely a conversation happening, though we couldn't hear it. Soon enough, Cece started walking towards the scene, too. I watched her brown braid bouncing as she moved quickly to her mate, and I wished she would come back. Both her and Chapman. They had gotten really comfortable with the aliens, and seemed to take no issue with walking right into dangerous situations with them. Chapman, at least, was a trained soldier. But Cece was a soft-hearted linguist.

"Those two, I tell ya," Kat said, shaking her shaved head, echoing my thoughts. Well, her head had once been shaved. She now had the beginnings of a micro pixie cut, her white-blonde hair coming in soft and short.

"I know," I said flatly. Luckily, Chapman and Cece's presence seemed to diffuse things further, and soon enough, the new guy and Buroudei lowered their blades. Chapman began to haul Gahn Fallo away, looking irritated as she often did with him, and Cece and Buroudei stayed back talking to the new guy. I felt my brows contract as I watched. *Why did they let him attack with no repercussions? Why are they just talking, now?* Cece looked pretty relaxed and was smiling. *Hmm.*

Then it hit me. *Of course.*

These men must have been from the third tribe that had agreed to come live here with us. So they weren't enemies. In fact, they were going to be our neighbours.

"But why did they attack...?" I said the question aloud without meaning to. The other girls began drifting away from the tent's opening now that the action seemed to have ended, and Kat and I were the only ones left.

"Please, it's Fallo," Kat said. "Dude probably has enemies from coast to fucking coast. Or desert to desert, I guess. Do you think this planet has any coasts?"

"Actually, it does." All of us had gotten sparse training related to our areas of expertise. As a geologist, I'd gotten some basic info about the planet and what we knew of its materials and makeup. Most of the planet was desert, mountain, and rock, but there was at least one dark sea that I knew of, its waters licking right up against the copper sand.

"Huh. Interesting. Alright, well, I'm heading to bed now that it looks like we're not all about to get shanked in our sleep. 'Night." Kat stood and moved to her bed of hides, leaving me alone at the tent's opening. I wasn't ready to stop watching yet. Wasn't ready to give up my vigilance so easily.

The circle of warriors who had been watching the fight dispersed, and Cece and Buroudei were walking away now, too, back towards Buroudei's tribe's area and their tents. The warrior who'd attacked stood alone on the sands, his large blade hanging from his strong grip. He was pretty far away, and I squinted harder, feeling drawn to take in every detail about him that I could.

He wasn't as tall as some of the other warriors I'd seen, but still was easily seven feet tall, and was frankly built like a fucking tank. He was wider of shoulder and thicker of thigh than some of the other men here, packed with heavy, corded muscle. His hair was unusual, cut bluntly at his shoulders and unbraided where most of the other men I'd seen wore theirs a lot longer. A flicker of recognition flashed in me. *I've only seen one other alien with hair cut like that...*

The man turned, heaving a heavy breath, and tipping his

head back to stare up at the starlit sky. I gasped, my heart rate immediately rocketing faster. It was him. The one from the battle. The one who'd locked his gaze onto me with an intensity I'd felt all the way down to my bones. The scarred one. The new Gahn of the mountain tribe.

Gahn Taliok.

He wasn't looking at me, now. I knew these guys had extremely sharp sight, smell, and hearing, but I doubted even at this distance he'd be able to see me in the shadows. Those shadows gave me a feeling of security as I worked to slow my breathing, leaning slightly forward.

The reflective asteroids and stars drenched Gahn Taliok in silver, lighting up every ripple of muscle. And every deep scar. My breath caught at the sight of them. Deep and angry, ripping down one side of his face, his neck, shoulder, and down his torso. Even his right ear hadn't escaped whatever damage had been done, and it hung bent and notched where the other was tall and pointed like the other men I'd seen.

Something about his scars seemed... off. They seemed out of place, unusual. No other warrior I'd seen had scars. Even Gahn Fallo, who'd almost got his damn head chopped off and had lost use of his arm for days, didn't have a single mark. None of us did, in fact, even those of us whose skin got really torn up on the irkdu our first day here. The Lavrika's blood had healed us as if there had never been a wound to begin with. So what the hell had happened to him?

My eyes trailed down Gahn Taliok's shining skin, picking over each scar like they were lines on a map. As if they could tell me something about this mysterious Gahn, the one whose eyes had tried to tear me open the last time I had seen him.

I drew my arms around my torso, pulling tightly into myself, my hackles rising. Yeah, those eyes had tried to tear me open, alright. They'd tried to get right inside me. But they hadn't succeeded. And they never would.

I felt every wall I'd ever built rising higher to keep him out. To keep them all out. But then his gaze shifted, focusing in on the tent, on the tent's opening, maybe even on *me*, and I felt all of those walls fucking *quake*. Dust cascaded, and a terrific, cracking boom ran through their foundations. I swallowed a choked cry and fell away from the opening, further back into the flickering darkness.

I closed my eyes, breathing deeply, trying to hold my walls steady, trying to keep it all together.

In my mind, my hands were ready. In one hand, I held a trowel, in the other, mortar.

Time to add more bricks.

4

TALIOK

As dawn's early light drifted through the air, I rose. I had not slept and did not wish to lay longer in that one spot.

Our small party had only brought simple bed hides and no tents, and we'd slept under the sky against a small dip in the cliff face. I'd arranged my bed so that I could maintain the new women's tent in my line of sight at all times. Knowing that my mate, my *Melanie*, as Zeezee had called her, was so close, but just out of reach, had been a hot stone under my skin all night. Not seeing her, coupled with my anger at not killing Gahn Fallo, had made sleep impossible.

The sun moved up on the horizon, chasing our broken moons away for the day, and I began strapping my weapons to my back. I'd kept some on during the night, of course, but Gahn Irokai's large blade, and a few others, were too big to sleep comfortably with. Not that I'd slept, anyway.

I glanced down at my men. Oxriel and the others slept soundly on their hides. Somewhere nearby our irkdu were roaming, or maybe sleeping, probably somewhere in the cliffs where their favourite peet grass grew.

I turned my gaze once again to the new women's tent. Their large tent was up against the cliff wall, in the centre of a large, scooped-out section of the cliff face. It was nestled and protected there, and I grunted in satisfaction at that. It was a good place. Safer than other areas of the cliffs, and certainly safer than the open sands.

With all my weapons and my loincloth in place, I began to walk, observing our new home. I moved away from the cliffs to get a better sense of the scale of everything.

In that large, concave area was the new women's tent. Out towards one end of the rounded-out area was a collection of tents. Not too many – likely Gahn Buroudei's tents. His tribe was much smaller than Fallo's. I kept scanning the scene to get my bearings. Opposite from Gahn Buroudei's tents, at the other end of the open area built into the cliffside, was a much larger settlement of tents. I felt my lips draw back from my teeth in an involuntary snarl. Fallo's tents.

I moved further out onto the open sands. The sun was painting the cliffside its usual warm, rich colour, lifting the blackness of the night. In the light, I could better see the cliff's many crags, openings, and protrusions. My tail lashed against the sand as I realized there was no good place left close to the tent of the new women for our tribe's tents. Buroudei's tents were on one side, Fallo's on the other. The only other place was between them, but that would be far too close to the other tribes and would offer the least amount of protection against predators who may come from out on the open sands.

I had few options. I could try to force either Gahn Buroudei or Gahn Fallo from their places, but that would undoubtedly end in violence, and then I would lose all access to the new women and my mate. I certainly could not set up in the open space between the two tribes. So that really only left finding another settlement area, further from the others. And further from the new women.

I growled to myself, flexing my clawed fingers. I was not used to this. Making decisions like this. My parents had died young, so I was used to making decisions regarding my own life. But this, deciding something for the entire tribe? It was much more difficult. I had to balance the needs of my many friends and tribe mates against my own desires to be as close to my mate as possible.

I glared at the new women's tent as if the power of my eyes could rip its fabric apart. As if by staring hard enough, I could call Melanie to me. Every instinct in me told me to take her away from the others, take her away from *everyone*, and make her mine. But she was not of our sands, and those were not her ways. My chest clenched when I remembered what Gahnala Zeezee had told me – that Melanie did not feel the sacred mate bond for me. I did not even think she spoke my language. For a moment, hopelessness threatened to overwhelm me, but I tore it down. I was Taliok, now Gahn of my people. I had killed the krixel that had killed my strong father when I was just a child. And then I'd dragged my father back to my people with only the strength of my own bleeding body. I would prevail. Against this, and all things.

But Melanie was not something to conquer. She was something to be won. To be won over. And I had no idea where to start.

I repeated my vow from last night. *I will learn. Everything I need to know about her and her people, I will learn.*

And I had one advantage on my side to help speed up the process. There were two warriors who had already won the love of their strange new mates. I had no interest in speaking to Fallo on this subject. The fact he'd won his new mate to him was likely pure black luck. Either that or his new

Gahnala was not entirely of sound mind. But there was one other Gahn I could speak to on the matter.

Raising my chin, I walked to Buroudei's tent.

Gahn Buroudei had just emerged from his tent for the morning as I approached. His tent was easy to find. Besides what I assumed to be the healers' tent, it was the largest in his small settlement. He raised his tail over his eyes when he saw me, and I did the same, a show of respect that helped ease some of the tension between us. My skin itched, and my tail jerked against the sand as I lowered it. I was not used to this, to being so close to other tribes, other Gahns, whom I had once considered my enemies. But at least Buroudei had proven himself a good ally in the past, though I still harboured some anger about him stopping my revenge last night.

"Greetings, Gahn Taliok," Buroudei said, tightening a belt around his waist.

My tail thumped in response. I had come here with a clear purpose, but now that I was here, I could not form the words to ask my questions. I was completely distracted from my original purpose, though, when I heard the snuffling sound of an animal in Buroudei's tent.

I whirled, drawing a blade at the sound: a great, rhythmic, snorting. It was unlike any predator I had ever heard before.

"Gahn Buroudei, where is your mate? There is a beast in your tent! Why do you not draw your blade?" I cried.

Buroudei's great mouth opened in a throaty laugh.

"It is no beast, Taliok, but the most beautiful creature to grace this world. That is my Gahnala, my Zeezee. She slumbers deeply, and she snorts as she does so," he said.

I stared at him, my blade still hanging in midair, caught between my clenched fists. The snorting sound split the air again, causing me to jump and jerk my head towards the sound. Buroudei's laughter got louder.

"You have many things to learn about the new women, Gahn Taliok," Buroudei chuckled. "I cannot tell a lie – I do hope to see you make that face and jump like that again when your own mate does something surprising."

I sheathed my weapon uneasily, trying to ignore the strange and terrible sound coming from Gahn Buroudei's tent.

"That cannot be normal," I muttered. "Are you sure she is not ill? Or deformed?"

No creature would breathe that laboriously in sleep if their nose and throat and lungs were properly made. I was sure of it.

Buroudei's smile vanished.

"She is exquisite in her perfection, Gahn Taliok, and you had better watch your foul tongues when you speak of her."

I grunted, even as another snorting sound made my teeth clench.

When he saw that I had no more ill words to speak of his Gahnala, Buroudei relaxed somewhat.

"What is it you've come here so early to speak of, Gahn Taliok?"

I sighed, glancing over at the new women's tent. So far, no one had emerged from it. I wondered, if I got closer, if I'd hear the other women snuffling like Zeezee was. Would my mate make such a sound?

If she did, I was sure it would be much easier on the ears than what I was hearing now.

"I have come to speak of... well... this." I gestured vaguely at his tent. "My ignorance of the new women. I want you to tell me how you made Zeezee... what did she say? Fall in love?"

Buroudei huffed.

"Ah, it was no easy task to win her love," he said gravely.

"Only a mighty Gahn can do such a thing. I will not pretend to tell you it will happen for you. Only the strongest, the best of men, can accomplish such a feat..."

I stared at him flatly as his face broke into a broad grin. Thankfully, the snorting sound in the background had faded, and I could focus more easily on Gahn Buroudei.

"No task is too great. Tell me what to do, and I will do it," I ground out. I felt like I was begging. I hated the feeling, but I would do it, do anything, for a chance to win my mate to me. My scars marred any chance I had at winning her with physical beauty. I would have to learn other ways.

Buroudei leaned in closer as if to tell me some great secret.

"Tongues, Taiok. Tongues."

"Tongues?" I repeated, like a fool. But I couldn't help it. I had no idea what he meant.

"Yes. Tongues," Gahn Buroudei continued. "Our people have three strong tongues. If you use them correctly, you can win your woman to you with the strength of those tongues alone."

My blood heated, and my fists clenched hard, claws biting into skin. I did not think Gahn Buroudei meant tongues as a metaphor for talking. What did he want me to do with my tongues? My tail thrashed in irritation. Was this something specific to the new women, or something to do with mates in general? I had never lain with one of my own kind and I had nothing to compare to and nothing to go on.

Buroudei was still smiling. *He is playing me for a fool.* And maybe I was a fool. But I did not have to act one, now, and take Buroudei's nonsense words to heart.

"You are useless," I muttered. "Get me someone who speaks plainly, and who knows of what they speak. Let me talk to your Gahnala."

Buroudei started to try to tell me no, that she was still sleeping, when a soft, groggy voice came from inside the tent.

"I'm awake, I'm awake. Hold on a *second.*"

A moment later she emerged wearing a long tunic and a strange, stiff cloak with a hood pulled up over her head. Shiny black shells covered her eyes, making them huge and insect-like, and her feet were wrapped in hard casings. I raised my tail before her, and she beamed.

Her smile faltered.

"Oh, *shoot,* still have to do my *sunscreen.* One *sec.*"

She went back inside the tent, then returned with an odd-looking blue tube in her hand. It looked sort of like it could be a plant, and when she squeezed it, bluish-white goo emerged, the way gel came from valok or talka plants when squeezed. She bent and began smearing the stuff on her bare legs. Buroudei knelt before her and began helping rub the white stuff into her skin. His hands looked huge against her small limbs.

"It's *sunscreen,*" she said again. She straightened as Buroudei continued to cover her legs with the thick goo. "Thanks. But keep your hands where I can see them, *mister,*" she said to him, down on his knees. He grunted and continued his work as she fixed her gaze on me again. At least, I assumed she did. It was impossible to see her eyes behind the shiny black shells.

"Humans are sensitive to the sun. It burns us, so we wear clothing like this, and use sunscreen to cover our skin," she said.

Was she treating me as a fool the way Buroudei had? Did she expect me to believe that the sun would actually harm someone?

But then again, why would she have all this clothing, and this *sunscreen,* if she were lying?

My suspicions mounted that she was deformed indeed. She could not breathe properly while sleeping, and needed all this equipment just to exist under the sun? It was unfathomable.

"Do all the women suffer from this affliction?" I asked, concerned. I imagined kneeling before Melanie, rubbing this thick stuff into her skin each morning. How soft would her skin be, beneath my claws?

"It's not an affliction, *jeez*. It's just how we are. We don't come from this world, you know."

"And your world has no sun?" I balked. I could not imagine such a thing.

Buroudei was finished and he stood, handing the blue tube back to Zeezee.

"Well, it does,' she said. "And the sun there can burn, too. But it's not as strong as this." She waved a small hand towards the sun. now higher in the sky and warming the sands, making everything glow.

I had so much to learn. About their world, their people. About Melanie. Melanie, whom I still had not seen since I'd come here. I had not seen her since the night of the battle beyond Fallo's hills. The night Gahn Irokai had died.

Unable to stop myself, I looked over at the new women's tent. A couple of the new women had ventured out, wearing the same strange cloaks as Zeezee, but I did not see Melanie among them. This unsettled me.

"Where is Melanie?"

My words came out harsh and guttural, and Buroudei gave a warning growl. Zeezee flapped her hand at him in an unfamiliar way, but one that seemed to be dismissive. And to my shock, he backed down, relaxing but looking at me sternly from behind her. The way Zeezee, and Chapman, had tamed their Gahns was the stuff of legends. Would I be the same way with my mate? Would I bend to every wave of her delicate hand? I suspected that yes, it would be so. But I would have to actually see her first to find out. And my patience was wearing thin.

"She's here. She's safe. You don't need to worry. She's probably sleeping or just getting dressed for the day. Relax," Zeezee said. She looked at me for a moment longer, rubbing her little chin with clawless fingers. Then she spoke again, "So, are you going to be this *grumpy* when you talk to her for the first time?"

"I do not know. What is *grumpy*?"

"Angry. Irritated. Annoyed. Annoying," she said. "Are you going to be all *growly* and *grumpy* when you approach Melanie? Because I don't think that's going to get you anywhere. In fact, it will probably make her run the other way."

If *grumpy* was as Zeezee described, then yes, I certainly felt *grumpy*.

"This is why I have come here in the first place," I huffed, forcing myself to keep my voice even. "I came to ask how to win Melanie's love to me, but Gahn Buroudei gave me nothing but useless advice about tongues."

Zeezee's face grew red beneath her cloak's hood, and she jerked her head back towards her mate, muttering, "Are you serious?"

Then she turned back to me, the sunlight glinting on her black shell eyes, and sighed.

"Come on. Let's take a walk together."

Buroudei made another dissatisfied sound, but one more vague flap of his mate's hand silenced him. He watched us darkly, tail swishing, as Zeezee began to walk away from their tent. Not wanting to lose my chance at whatever information Zeezee had to offer, immediately I followed.

We walked through the tents of Buroudei's tribe. All around us, people of the Sea Sands raised their tails as we passed. Zeezee smiled and called out greetings to all she encountered. I could see that she was already a well-loved Gahnala. I could also see that Gahn Buroudei was following us from a distance, but I ignored him. I could not blame him for that. No true warrior would let his mate go with a rival Gahn alone if he could help it.

As we passed the tent of the new women, I could not help but stare at it, willing Melanie to appear. But she did not. And perhaps it was better that way. I was not yet prepared to face her. I had not yet learned all I needed to learn from Zeezee.

Zeezee led us to a secluded outcropping of stone that created a shaded nook. She stepped into the shadows and pushed her black shells up over her forehead. She squinted at me appraisingly, and I set my jaw. I did not flinch under her gaze. I had nothing to be ashamed of and nothing to hide. But I could not help the slight sting of heat when her eyes passed over my scars.

"Why do you have scars?" she blurted. "Nobody else does, and they all chop each other up on a regular basis."

I stiffened.

"It is a long story I do not wish to tell."

Zeezee regarded me another long moment, then nodded.

"No problem. Alright, ask away. What questions do you have for me?"

I grunted tilting my head.

"I thought that was obvious. I want to learn how to make Melanie fall in love with me." The fact that Melanie did not already feel the sacred mate bond was a spreading pain in my ribs.

"OK, first of all, lose the attitude," Zeezee said. "You're not going to win her over like that."

My heart sank. Already, I was failing, and I hadn't even met her yet.

"Teach me, Gahnala. Tell me what to do."

It was a broken-sounding plea, but I was past the point of caring.

"There's no single way to make a woman fall in love with you," she said. "There are some things you can do, though, that will help your chances."

"What things?"

"Like, well, talking to her, for one."

I stared at her, disbelieving. This was the great wisdom of the human Gahnala?

"I... am not good at talking," I finally replied. Action had always been, in my mind, far superior to conversation. Could I not prove myself and win Melanie's love through some great act? Like the baklok, the tournament sometimes used to choose a new Gahn, but instead to make Melanie fall in love?

"*God*, you and Melanie are going to be two *peas in a pod*, I tell you," Zeezee said with an odd shake of her head.

What are peas and why are they in a pod? Wait, what is a pod?

This was not helping. I was more confused than before.

Maybe I should have just followed my instincts. Maybe I should go to the tent, now, take her in my arms and go far away from here.

I did not do it. Instead, I raked my claws through my loose hair, gnashing my fangs.

"I do not understand."

Zeezee's face softened in what looked to be sympathy. Or maybe pity.

"I know you don't," she said. "We still have a lot to learn about each other. I was just saying before that you and Melanie are a lot alike. She also doesn't talk much."

What a relief.

Not that I did not want to hear Melanie speak. I wanted to hear every word she had ever said to anyone, and keep them all for myself. But if it was going to be as confusing as talking to Zeezee, then keeping it to a minimum might have been best.

My tail swished and I said, "This is good."

Zeezee raised a slim eyebrow.

"Don't be so sure," she said, and once again, my heart sank. I was already not sure. Zeezee did not have to tell me to be *less* sure.

"She's going to be a tough *nut* to crack." When she saw my face, she shook her head so vigorously that it looked like it would make her dizzy. "Sorry. Another human expression. It just means it will be hard to get her to open up. She doesn't share much with anyone. She's very private and quiet. Not to say that she isn't wonderful – she is. She's super smart and a great, loyal friend. But I think you might find it hard to close the distance between you."

Distance. What could such a thing mean when my mate had already travelled from another world entirely, out from beyond the stars? But now that she was here, mere steps from me, she felt further away than ever.

"Oh, God, don't look so hopeless," Zeezee cried.

Had I looked hopeless?

"The Lavrika obviously knows what it's doing," she continued. "But you're going to have to work for it, I think. And that will start by talking to her."

The sacred mate bond of our people was so much more efficient than this. There was little need for talking. Because it was all *feeling*.

But Melanie felt nothing for me.

Yet.

"What should we talk about?"

"Anything!" Cece replied, completely unhelpfully. "Get to know her. Talk about whatever comes to mind."

I tried to be grateful for Zeezee's help, but so far it didn't feel much like help. An unfamiliar anxiety gripped me, and I found myself flexing and curling my fingers, over and over again.

"Speak of the *devil*! There she is. Why don't you go practise talking to her, now?"

My heart charged in my chest so hard it was a wonder it did not break through my skin. I whipped around to face back towards the tents, my eyes rolling frantically over the scene.

There was a small group of human women outside their tent, now. But even with their coverings and their eye shells, I spotted my mate right away. It was impossible not to. My gaze was drawn to her as if by some invisible force. She crouched at the edge of the group, fingering what looked to be a small stone. When another woman spoke to her, she dropped it and stood.

She is all reserved grace.

I was thunderstruck by her. Even at this distance, I drank in the perfection of her face, ravenous for her, memorizing every detail as if I hadn't already memorized it at the pools of the Lavrika. When she smiled at the friend who had spoken to her, it was only a brief flicker. But a beautiful flicker, all the same. I felt the beauty of it so hard, I could practically taste it. She overwhelmed every sense. Pounded in every stretch of my scarred body.

A sharp, agonizing recognition exploded inside me, as if everything I was, everything I had ever been, and ever would be, existed only for her, now. A great pull tugged, deep in my abdomen, urging me forward. This sensation was only made stronger when Zeezee gave me a small shove.

I repeated Zeezee's advice to myself.

Talk to her. Talk to her.

But couldn't she see, couldn't they all see, that that would be impossible, now?

It would be impossible to speak to my mate.

Because in that moment, I was certain that I'd forgotten every single word I'd ever learned. My tongues were stuck fast. My head was empty.

But my heart was achingly full.

5

MELANIE

"Find anything good, Geo Girl?"

I dropped the pebble I'd been studying and stood, smiling briefly at Kat who'd just spoken to me. We had just emerged from the tent and joined Theresa, Serena, and a couple of other girls after getting dressed for the day.

"Not sure," I replied honestly. Kat and I had decided on a self-appointed project – we were looking for ways to create a natural sunscreen from the materials on this planet. The sunscreen we'd brought from Earth wouldn't last forever. Between her chemistry expertise and my background in geology, we figured we could do it. But so far I hadn't found anything that might contain a compound like zinc oxide or titanium dioxide which we used in natural sunscreens on Earth.

"Come on," Kat said. "We're gonna go pee."

I dusted my hands off on my pants, pulling my hood a little closer against the sun, already so hot this early in the morning. Despite the heat, I felt a small shiver. I rolled my shoulders uncomfortably as that shiver moved down my spine. My skin prickled, and instinctively I hunched a little more into myself. *Someone's watching me.*

I didn't have time to ruminate on the feeling, because soon we were moving. I was glad to get away from that spot. But the feeling of being watched followed.

Our small group headed away from the tent and towards the cliff, looking for what had become a familiar crack in its jagged wall. That crack opened into a kind of stone hallway that led to a sandy clearing that we'd designated as the human pee-zone. We got to the clearing and quickly did our business in the sand, covering everything over like cats in a giant litter box.

As we left the cliffs and moved back towards the tent, the sound of my name made me jerk my head.

"Melanie!"

Cece was grinning from beneath her hood and sunglasses, waving to me as she strode over. I stopped, and the other girls continued on their way, heading to whatever tasks they were working on today – weaving bandages, airing out hides, or helping the Sea Sand people with other chores.

"Hey," I said, letting a small smile touch my lips again. Cece had been one of my roommates on the spaceship, along with Kat and Theresa, and I considered her one of my closest friends now. We didn't know a whole lot about each other, but in a place like this, so far from home, that sort of thing didn't seem to matter all that much. "What's up?" I added as she stopped before me, hands on her hips.

Her smile faltered a little, and her voice got quiet.

"Well, honestly, I came here to warn you."

I shivered again and wrapped my arms around myself.

"Warn me of what?"

My voice was hard and low, and Cece backtracked, shaking her head and waving her hands in front of her.

"Sorry, that may have sounded really serious. I'm just here to give you a little heads up."

She looked away from me then, and I followed her gaze, sucking in a breath as it landed on the huge, scarred alien who'd attacked Gahn Fallo last night. The one who'd stared at me on the battlefield. He was staring at me again, now, from a little ways down the cliff, and I finally placed the source of that unnerving sensation of being watched.

It's him.

"That idiot," Cece muttered under her breath, watching him. "I was trying to get him to come over here to talk to you himself, but he won't. He wasn't ready, or something. He didn't exactly say, but I think he's shy."

I had no fucking clue what Cece was muttering away to herself about, but the assertion that this warrior alien, the one who charged into battle like it was nothing, was *shy*, made me laugh out loud. Cece turned back towards me at the sound, her brows raised in surprise. I coughed a little as my laugh died down. I hadn't laughed like that in a long time. But it just seemed so... absurd. Calling a hulking, huge, scarred warrior like that shy.

"I'm serious!" Cece said, looking indignant before dissolving into giggles herself. "I think he's shy! He won't come talk to you!"

"And why does he need to come talk to me in the first place?" I asked, growing uneasy once again. What did Cece want to warn me about?

"Ah, right, well that's what I came over here to tell you. I don't know if he wants me to do this but I didn't want you feeling unprepared or out of the loop for whenever he finally pulls his head out of his ass and comes over. I know that not everyone is as comfortable with this whole arrangement as Chapman and me."

Arrangement? What arrangement?

46

Chapman and me.

The only women who had alien mates.

Oh, God. No. No no no.

I knew what Cece was going to say before she said it, but the words that came next still felt like a punch to the gut.

"Gahn Taliok saw your face in the Lavrika pools before we arrived here. The Lavrika told him you're meant to be his mate."

My heart dropped down to the pit of my stomach, and I swear it would have gone lower if every muscle and sphincter in my body hadn't gone tighter than the skin of a snare drum.

"That's not possible," I said, shaking my head fiercely. I was cold again, but sweating now. She was damn right that not everyone was as comfortable with this whole mate thing as her and Chapman. I had no problem with them getting their alien thang on, and I didn't judge them for their attractions like some of the girls, but I also wasn't about to jump into bed with one, either. Especially one who hovered like a goddamn creeper, staring at me like he wanted to burn a hole through my body with his eyes. I licked my lips, my mouth suddenly so dry, glancing over at him again. Our eyes met, and the already tense-looking alien stiffened further. I swallowed, hard, worried he was about to charge at me the way he had Gahn Fallo. But he didn't. Instead, he heaved a huge breath, turned his massive body, and quickly walked away, tail whipping behind him.

"What the fuck? I told him to come here and talk to you! And he said he wanted my help..." Cece crossed her arms, watching Gahn Taliok's retreating figure with furrowed brows. I blew out a sigh of relief. I'd gotten pretty used to the aliens we'd been with, but I knew next to nothing about Gahn Taliok. Aside from the fact that both times he'd shown up it had been to attack.

Cece turned back to me and placed a gentle hand on my shoulder.

"Buroudei told me that a man won't force a woman to be his mate, just so you know. From what he's told me, rape basically doesn't exist in their culture. They value the Lavrika's mate bond, but they also value women's choices. Even if those choices have caused some issues in the past."

Ah, right. Cece had told us about the aliens' unique biology. How a man could only father children of one gender, and that the aliens' ancestors had started forgoing the Lavrika's mate bond in order to pair with men who would give them sons. But when that had decimated their population, and left the genders wildly unbalanced, they had returned to the Lavrika's ways, staying with the mate they felt the bond with.

That was all well and fucking good for them. But I didn't plan on marrying an alien warlord just because the magic Cupid dragon had told Gahn Taliok I'd be a good wifey. I sincerely appreciated everything the aliens had done for us. In many ways, they'd been more supportive than my own family. And I was so grateful for the Lavrika giving all of us the gift of language, and for healing us with its magic milky blood. But that wasn't going to make me just accept its decision. I liked to be consulted on the course of my own life, thank you very much. That hadn't happened enough for me on Earth, and it certainly hadn't happened when I'd been yanked off my own planet and brought here.

I hadn't said anything to Cece, and she was looking at me with concern, now.

"I didn't mean to freak you out. Like I said, I wanted you to have the heads up. You know I and the other girls will support you no matter what, and you don't have to entertain the attentions of any guy you don't want. But for what it's worth..."

My eyes narrowed.

"For what it's worth," she continued, "I think he's a good guy. He's all tense and broody and awkward, but these guys grew up with very few women. I don't think he even knows how to talk to one of his own species, let alone a girl from another planet. But he has been a good ally to Buroudei."

"An ally? You mean when he and Gahn Buroudei attacked us?"

That battle was long over, but I still remembered the chaos and confusion of it. The way Gahn Fallo had almost died, and the way some of the other men *actually* had died, when Taliok and Buroudei had charged into Fallo's territory. Cece flinched, and her green eyes flashed.

"That wasn't an attack out of nowhere. We thought you guys needed to be rescued. Gahn Taliok put his own life at great risk, and lost his own Gahn, to try to help you guys. And me. All of us."

I stared at her, frowning. She was right. I knew it. Gahn Taliok and Gahn Buroudei had thought we weren't safe with Gahn Fallo and had wanted to reunite all of us. It had been a rescue mission from their perspective. But how much of Gahn Taliok's participation in that rescue was some noble sense of wanting to help, and how much of it was because he thought he'd score a human girl to take back to his tent?

"Well, thank you for the warning. Maybe you should go give *him* a warning now. Tell him that I'm not interested."

Cece smiled softly.

"I can do that if you want me to."

I chewed my lip, thinking, then shook my head. This wasn't middle school. I didn't need her to be my messenger. I could tell the guy myself. If Cece was right, and he really was a good guy, then I could give him that much. *Maybe he'll never even come talk to me anyway.* My eyes flicked back to the spot he'd been standing, but he was gone now, and I hadn't seen where he'd ended up.

"It's OK. I can handle my own stuff. I appreciate it, though," I said.

Cece squeezed my shoulder again then bounded away towards Gahn Buroudei's people's tents. I noticed Gahn Buroudei standing and watching, waiting for her. When she reached him, she launched into his arms, and I sighed. I was happy for her joy. Truly. I just didn't trust it. And I definitely didn't trust that kind of happiness for myself. *No, if Gahn Taliok tries something, I'll tell him no. I just want to keep my head down and survive here.*

It turned out it was kind of hard to just keep your head down when one of the alien kings spent most of the day staring at you from one random spot or another. Throughout the day I caught glimpses of him, from the cliffs or between tents, watching. Always watching. And it was starting to get on my nerves.

So that night when I emerged from the cliffs after peeing and found him about ten feet away, his eyes glued to me, I sighed, and then spoke, loudly enough for him to hear.

"Are you going to just keep staring like that?"

He stood straighter at my words, as if he hadn't expected to be addressed. I crossed my arms, watching him warily. My words had come out more confrontational than I'd intended, but there was no going back, now. *Wasn't I just thinking about how we shouldn't antagonize the aliens?* They'd offered us food, shelter, protection. But I couldn't go on like this. The feeling of hidden eyes on me all day made me want to scream.

Gahn Taliok was silent. God, he really was huge. While he wasn't as tall as the tallest warriors, he was a pure mountain of muscle, and still had more than a solid foot and a half of height on me. The only movement was the swish of his tail behind him in the sand in the darkness. Otherwise, he was like stone. Stone in the shape of a warrior. Stone that had been cracked and mangled and scarred. I couldn't help but let my eyes trace over those scars again. They were deep and ragged and dark grey against the coppery warmth and deeper browns of his skin. *What happened to you?*

He finally spoke, his voice deep and gruff. I gasped, my eyes shooting back up to his face at the sound.

"Does it bother you?"

I blinked.

Um. That's not the response I was expecting.

I had expected him to either deny that he'd been watching me or to make me feel like I was crazy and overreacting for calling him out on it. That's what humans I knew on Earth would have done. What my shitty ex-boyfriend Greg would have done.

But this? This calm acknowledgement of his actions, and asking me about my feelings on it? I was not expecting that at all.

I was suspicious, but I answered honestly, figuring that if he got angry with my answer I could scream. The other women in the tent nearby would hear me, not to mention the other hundred warriors who had set up camp here.

"Yes. It does."

I watched him closely, heart pounding, looking for any sign of anger at my words, ready to turn and run. But apart from another swish of his tail, he made no move. A low grunt rumbled from his chest.

"Then I apologize."

A long moment stretched between us. Unsure what else to do, I finally settled on murmuring an awkward, "Alright."

But then suddenly, he was coming towards me, his gigantic body moving faster than I would have thought possible, striding with liquid grace over the sands. Instinctively, I stepped backwards, but I collided with the cliff wall.

He stopped before me, standing a pace away, and I felt my eyes widen as I took him all in. This close, his hugeness was inescapable. Quiet power radiated off of him in dark waves. That power rolled over me, crowding me against the stone of the cliffs, even though he was barely within arm's reach. He'd left space between us, but it didn't feel that way. My breath caught in my throat. Everything buzzed.

"I am sorry. I did not mean to bother you."

I flinched, unable to help it, at the deep growl of his voice. We had let the silences stretch out between us for so long that his words, when they came, were a shock to the system. And even more shocking? The actual words he was saying. *Sorry to bother you.* If my ex had said those words, they would have been whiny and sarcastic. A fake apology, meant to make me feel guilty. But I could sense no trace of that in Gahn Taliok. Just gruff sincerity.

Another long silence. *What am I supposed to say to that? I've already told him it's alright. Time to just move on and let this be.*

But then again, maybe I should tell him I don't plan on being his girlfriend or mate or wife or whatever. Nip whatever this is in the bud.

I took a shaky breath to tell him just that when he spoke again. And his next words stunned me into silence.

"It is never my intention to do anything but please you."

At first glance, he looked very still after he spoke. But I noticed a subtle flexing and tightening of his clawed fingers by his sides, and then the slight jump of a muscle in his hard jaw. The glimmering shards of his eyes pulsed, then drew inwards, hard, focusing in on me. In the starlit darkness, they looked like quicksilver. Mercury. I couldn't look away. They were pulling me in...

Before I could fall completely into that alien gaze, Gahn Taliok broke eye contact, gazing out to where the evening fire in Gahn Fallo's area was dying down.

"I apologize. I was doing it again," he gritted out, jaw working. He looked down and fixed his gaze on the sand before spinning and turning his back on me. My eyes slid over the tight bunch of thick muscles along his broad shoulders and down his strong back. Even his back was scarred. For an absurd moment, I wanted to reach out and trace those scars with my fingertips. I clenched my fists. *Pull it together.*

Gahn Taliok turned his head, just slightly, so that I could see his profile in the darkness, lit up by the asteroids and stars. The blunt ends of his hair thick black hair brushed his shoulders as he spoke.

"I will leave you now. Goodnight, Melanie from beyond the stars."

And with that, he was gone, stalking away over the dark sands, leaving me to wonder just what, exactly, the *fuck* had just happened.

6

TALIOK

T hough it pains me. Though it pains me.
Those were the words inside my head now. The unspoken ones to follow what I'd said out loud.

I will leave you now. Though it pains me.

And it was a true pain. Cold and biting. The ache of absence. It was worse than the tear of the krixel's claws who'd killed my father and scarred me so badly.

It pained me, but the alternative was even more unbearable. Being near Melanie, and not touching her. It had taken a great force of will to stop myself from reaching out and brushing her long, dark hair away from her lovely face with my claws. From running the pad of my thumb over her pink lips. I was not used to this agitation. This attraction. This powerful, terrible pull.

I felt it now, stronger and stronger with every step that took me away from her. Of course, I did not go far. I stopped a little ways down the cliff, then turned and watched to make sure she returned to the human tent safely. I did my best not to stare, for now I knew it bothered her. Instead, I watched her halfway, from the corner of my eyes, and strained my other senses, my hearing, my sense of scent, to follow her with those if not with my eyes.

When Melanie had safely returned to the large tent for the night, I relaxed slightly. But only slightly. Speaking with her had confirmed that she did not feel the sacred mate bond as I did. I was not accustomed to the new women's features, but everything in her face and body had spoken of wariness and mistrust.

That was not ideal.

How would I rectify such a thing? I thought about asking Zeezee again, but she would likely tell me to talk to Melanie more. The thought was a difficult one. Speaking to her had been a wounding thrill. Her voice was like a spear, right through my skin. Soft yet painful. I wanted to hear it again. And yet I did not know what else to say to coax it forth. She had not spoken freely to me just now. She had only spoken to answer my questions. And I did not know how to change that.

Oxriel's voice shook me from my thoughts, and I looked up to see him approaching.

"The rest of the tribe will be here soon. Have you decided where you want us to settle?"

I suppressed a groan. It had not been easy to determine an area for settlement. Every safe, comfortable area was too far from the new women. And the only places near to the new women were too close to the other tribes, or too exposed to the open sands. But I had made my decision.

"I have," I said. "Come. I will show you."

I turned, and Oxriel followed. With the options I had, I had chosen the safer area that was further from the new women. It made me want to gnash my fangs in anger, but I could not put all of my tribe at risk by living too close to Gahn Fallo, or too exposed to the open sands with their scuttling zeelk.

Oxriel and I walked out of the large scooped-out section of the cliff that housed the new women in the middle and Fallo and Buroudei's tribes on either side. We trekked along the cliffs until we reached another similar, but much smaller divot. It was not a wide opening in the cliff, but the clearing went deep and offered ample space and protection for our small tribe. We had only half the numbers of Fallo, and our tents and supplies would do well here.

Oxriel and I entered the area. He looked around the dark space and swished his tail in satisfaction.

"It is very good, Gahn. Our people will be safe here. And the high rock walls will remind them of our mountains."

Safe, certainly. But happy?

The others may have been. But already I felt so far, too far, from Melanie. Knowing that the rival Gahns were so close to her, while we were out here, was a zeelk spur in my guts. But it could not be avoided.

If only I'd gotten here sooner, before Fallo. Then the Mad Gahn and his people would be relegated to this tiny, distanced crack in the cliff instead of us.

The moon drenched the dark sand around my feet like blood.

Maybe I should just kill him after all.

No. No. that would make everything worse. I had to lay my vengeance down and lay it down forever. For Melanie.

I realized I had not responded to Oxriel, and I grunted.

"We will sleep here tonight. Tell the others to bring their bedding hides here."

Oxriel raised his tail over his eyes, then left, heading back towards the small spot on the outskirts of the settlement where the five of us had been sleeping so far. Soon enough he and my other three warriors would return, and sometime soon, likely tomorrow, the rest of our tribe would arrive. We would be starting a new life for our people here. Everything was changing. The new women had changed it.

I did not know if all these changes would be good or bad, but I did not dwell on it. The changes had come and would continue to come whether I liked it or not. All that was left was to face them.

I crouched, then sat, crossing my ankles and resting my hands on my knees tipping my face up to the sky. The stars were different here than they were in my mountains. Everything was slightly out of place.

It did not unnerve me.

I did not doubt my decision to come here. Not even for a moment.

I did wonder, sometimes, if Gahn Irokai might have done things differently.

But it was no matter. He was dead now.

And there was only me.

7

MELANIE

I woke up the next morning to Theresa shaking my shoulder. I rolled onto my back and squinted as her brown eyes and blond hair came into focus above me.

"Wake up, girl, the rest of the new aliens are here!"

Kat groaned loudly from beside us, burrowing deeper into her hides.

"Wow, more aliens. Big whoop," she grumbled.

Theresa rolled her eyes at our grumpy friend, then turned her attention back to me.

"Come on. Don't you wanna check them out? See what their deal is?"

I sat up and nodded, rubbing my eyes. I did want to check them out. I wanted to get a sense of who else would be living near us. I nudged Kat with my elbow.

"You should come too," I said. "We should make sure we know who we're living with."

She gave another groan.

"I can already tell you what they'll be like," she replied. "They're gonna be mostly guys, more than seven feet tall, and are going to look like some kind of nightmare kangaroos. If they're not like that, if they look like pigeons or hamsters or some other shit, then you can come wake me up to see."

Kat said nothing more, a silent lump among her hides. Theresa and I shrugged at each other. I dressed quickly, pulling on my grey pants, tank top, solar protection jacket, and sunglasses. Theresa and I helped each other smear sunscreen on our faces. Without mirrors, we needed each other to see if we d missed any spots. When we were ready to go, we headed outside to join the rest of the human girls, watching from outside the tent in a clump.

This was the first time we had seen an arrival like this. Last time, we had been the ones arriving with Gahn Fallo's people. Gahn Buroudei's people had already been settled here. To the left of the human tent, I saw Cece, Gahn Buroudei, and his people waiting. To the right was Gahn Fallo, Chapman, and the rest of that tribe. We were smack dab in the middle. And straight ahead of us was the new tribe, moving slowly over the sands towards the cliffs, riding on irkdu.

Between us and the newcomers stood Gahn Taliok and the four men he'd come with. A strange heat flooded through me at the sight of him, and memories of last night came rushing back – memories of questions and apologies and sincerity so deep it practically burned. I licked my lips, looking at his muscled back, lined with weapons, then tore my gaze away. *Who's staring now?* Gahn Taliok didn't seem to have noticed me. And why should he have? He was far away with his back to me. And I had given him no reason to look my way again.

Good. It's good that he's not looking.

So why did that thought feel so damn hollow?

As the newcomers reached the outer limits of the new settlement, Gahn Taliok began to walk away, out over the sands and then away down the cliffs. His four warriors, and then the irkdu with all his people, followed.

"Where are they goin'?" Theresa asked, peering after them.

"Not sure," I said honestly. "But it's kind of crowded in this area. Maybe they're going to set up further down the cliff."

For some reason that felt... weird. It felt weird that Gahn Taliok's people had to be so far away. Like it was somehow unfair.

Unfair? I thought. *Girl, you are being crazy.*

Soon enough, the whole new tribe had disappeared, hidden by the curve of the cliffs, and the crowds watching and waiting dispersed.

"Sorry I woke you up for that," Theresa said, frowning. "Kinda anticlimactic."

"No, it's OK. Thanks. I'm glad I was here for it." I was glad to have gotten a glimpse of them, even a brief one. Gahn Taliok's tribe seemed to be roughly the same size as Gahn Buroudei's. About fifty people total, mostly young men, with some women, children, and elderly aliens. Gahn Fallo's tribe was by far the largest, but Taliok and Buroudei's people together rivalled his numbers. *I guess that's why they had to ally against him for the battle.*

After a bathroom break and some dried meat and valok gel, the stuff that came from the inside of the funny little cactus plants that seemed to grow everywhere, I was ready to start my day, and I began it the same way I always did. At the cliff wall, chipping away at the stone, examining pebbles, and digging down through the sand. I was trying to get a handle on the materials of this planet. It helped me feel grounded. And it made me feel productive since I was looking for something to help Kat come up with a sunscreen concoction.

The fact that I'd found absolutely nothing useful yet was beside the point.

At least I'm doing something.

I was alone, but not far from the others. I was roughly halfway between the human tent and Gahn Fallo's area. I could hear some human voices from the area of our tent, but most of the other girls were hanging out with the women we'd made friends with in Gahn Fallo's territory – Bokeelie, Anata, Vola, and the other women and their kids. Most of the men, from both Gahn Buroudei and Gahn Fallo's tribes, were out hunting or patrolling or visiting their old territory. I wondered how the new tribe was doing, in their alcove so far from here.

You don't need to worry about it. They're doing just fine.

I spent the next few hours poking at rocks and running my fingers through dust. I stopped for a quick lunch break, then went right back to it. But it wasn't long after I'd eaten that I became aware of a presence behind me. I froze, my hand tightening on the fist-sized rock I held. I subtly lifted my chin to look up from the rock in my hand to the cliff face. The sun was behind me, and I could see a huge shadow on the wall beside my own crouching one, distorted by the jagged rock surface. One of the shadow's ears was lopsided and bent.

Gahn Taliok.

I breathed out slowly. Even though I wasn't keen on this whole *you're my mate* thing, I was somewhat glad it was him. After last night, I felt like I knew him at least a little bit. Sort of. I mean, it wasn't like I *really* knew him, or truly trusted him, but he didn't feel so much like a stranger now.

"What are you doing back there?" I asked, without turning around.

"I'm not staring." His voice was a deep ripple, right down

my spine. I stiffened, and swallowed, before turning my head back to look at him over my shoulder.

"I can see that," I replied. He wasn't lying. In fact, it looked like he was trying very hard to look anywhere but at me. His gaze was focused on the cliff wall above my head.

He didn't say anything else, and I sighed again.

"You might not be staring. But you are hovering."

Gahn Taliok jerked his gaze down, staring at his feet.

"But my feet are on the ground."

His words were half a statement, half a question, and I couldn't help but shake my head at his confusion. There was something oddly charming about the communication barrier, the way he seemed to take some things so literally without the human context to understand.

"Nevermind," I said. I moved from my crouch to a sitting position, spinning my butt in the sand to face him. He looked even more giant than normal, towering over me while I sat at his feet. Not liking the feeling, I immediately stood, brushing the sand and dust from my pants.

Standing was a lot better than sitting, but I still felt really, really tiny, and really, really powerless next to him.

When Gahn Taliok spoke next, once again his voice went right down my fucking spine, but this time it sank all the way down, deep into my pelvis, making me draw a hard breath.

"What are *you* doing?" he asked.

"Me?" I repeated. Like an idiot. But the reversal of my question surprised me. I hadn't expected him to stay here and try to make conversation with me. "Um, well, I'm looking at the rocks."

"The rocks." Now it was Gahn Taliok's turn to repeat my words. His gaze was still lingering above my head, and I found that that was bothering me even more than his staring had.

"You can look at me, you know. Especially if we're

having a conversation. Most humans find it polite to make eye contact when speaking to someone." I pushed my sunglasses up to rest on top of my head under my hood, squinting.

His gaze didn't detach from the cliff.

"Most?"

I nodded.

"Well, a lot of people like to make eye contact when speaking, yeah. Some people find it uncomfortable, though, or prefer not to. For different reasons," I explained.

"Do you find it uncomfortable?"

I remembered back to last night when I'd practically fallen headfirst into those strange, silver shards of his eyes. I realized I was dying to know what colour his eyes were in the daylight.

"No," I finally blurted, shocked at myself. Yesterday I'd been telling him to stop looking at me, now I was practically begging him to look in my eyes? I needed to get my head on straight, and fast.

The moment I'd spoken, his gaze wrenched downward, capturing my own. As our eyes met, he seemed to get larger, get closer. Except he didn't. Other than shifting his gaze, he didn't move at all.

Once again, he'd left a decent amount of space between us. If I reached out from where I stood, I doubted my fingertips would be able to brush against his muscled abdomen. But I could see his large, dark eyes easily. In fact, they were all I could see.

The aliens' eyes, like everything about them, were larger than humans'. And they were black, with no white parts at all. Instead of a round iris or pupil, they had shimmering sparks, sight stars, that pulsed and moved like little universes. Those sparks that had looked silver last night, I realized now, were actually a surprisingly warm, gold colour.

The warmth I saw there felt at odds with his gruff demeanour and his dark scars.

I didn't know how much time had passed when Gahn Taliok spoke again, his voice rasping.

"When I first saw your face in the Lavrika's pools, I thought your white eyes were terrible. They were so different from my own. From anything I had ever seen."

Wow. You really know how to charm a girl, I thought. Cece had been right. This guy was totally clueless about how to approach women. But then again, I guess I couldn't really fault his honesty. I probably *had* looked terrible and alien to him, just as when we'd first arrived, they had all looked terrible and alien to us. And I would take honesty over false flattery any day.

"But now that you are here," he continued, a look of pained hunger darkening his face, "I see less of what makes us different and more of what makes us the same. Your eyes are not just white. They are also dark. Like mine."

I mean... I guessed he was right. I did have dark brown eyes, with black pupils. But they didn't have any gorgeous, glittering shards of gold in them. They were just plain old brown.

Hold on. Gorgeous? When had I started calling any part of this stalker gorgeous?

I was getting into dangerous territory. This was the first time Gahn Taliok had brought up the fact that I was supposed to be his mate, and he seemed to be trying to say something with this whole eye thing. Exactly what that was, I wasn't sure. And I wasn't exactly sure I wanted to find out either. No, what I wanted now was to get out of this situation as fast as possible.

Tell him. Tell him now. Tell him you're not interested in this whole fated mates thing...

He must have sensed my growing panic, because he tore his gold sight stars from my face, down to my hands.

"Tell me why you look at rocks."

"Huh?" I looked down, too, realizing I was still holding the rock I'd had from before. I tossed it down, reeling from his sudden change of the subject. But I was also relieved to have the conversation moving back into more neutral territory. "Oh. Um. That's what I do. Back home, where I come from, I was training to be a geologist."

"What is a *geologist*?"

Gahn Taliok's eyes had found their way to my face again, and I felt my cheeks heat for some stupid reason. I cleared my throat, ignoring the way that the earnest furrow of his brows was almost cute. At least, it would have been cute if it weren't on the massive alien killing machine who apparently wanted to make me his wife.

"It's someone who studies rocks and minerals." I replied. "It's their job. It's... it's like their life's work." Damn, it was a bit hard to explain the idea of a career to an alien who spent his days hunting and fighting and trying, very awkwardly, to woo human women.

Not human women, I reminded myself silently.

Human woman. Singular.

Hmm. It was probably a bad sign that I was so hung up on that. Hung up on the idea that he wasn't looking at any of the other women. Just me.

It's just because I want to protect my friends and keep them safe, I thought hurriedly. *Right?*

Gahn Taliok appeared to be digesting what I'd said.

"Why do you want to be a geologist? Why do you want to look at rocks all day?" he asked.

I tensed, hackles rising, ready to defend myself against his judgment. But as I looked at his frowning face, his focused, serious expression, I saw there was no judgment there. Just a deep, almost desperate need to understand what I'd said. To understand what I wanted. To understand *me*.

It was a completely foreign sensation. The feeling of someone sincerely listening, wanting to understand my thoughts and feelings. My parents had never afforded me anything close to this, and neither had my ex. I almost wanted to laugh, but bitterly. The person who'd attempted to understand me more than anyone else from my old life wasn't even a person at all, but an alien.

He's still a person. The thought came sharp and sudden. *Just because he isn't a human doesn't mean he isn't a person.*

And that alien, that person, was watching me now, his face just as serious as ever, waiting for me to speak as if what I was about to say was as important as the key to the meaning of life.

No pressure.

I cleared my throat a little, glancing at the rock I'd thrown down to the sand.

"Rocks are... stable," I began. "They're constant. I mean, yes, they change, but that can take millions of years. Rock and stone and landscape... It's all so rooted, so tied to history. I like how if you dig deep enough, you can literally see into the past. You can understand what's come before, and even get a sense of what may come in the future."

I was babbling now. I didn't think I'd said that many words in a row since I'd come to this planet. And maybe even before then. What was this guy's deal? Why was I telling him so much?

His brow had furrowed deeper, if that was even possible. The expression was slightly asymmetrical – the scars on the injured side of his face kept that eyebrow from pulling as far down as the other.

"You speak truly? You can tell things of the past, and even of the future, by looking at rocks?"

"More or less. If we look for the right patterns," I said.

"You are..." Gahn Taliok's voice trailed off as his golden sight stars exploded, swirling in dizzying patterns across his dark eyes. I watched them with guarded wonder until he continued, "...brilliance. You are brilliance."

My mouth fell open, and I snapped it shut instantly.

I started shaking my head, hard. I wasn't brilliance. I wasn't even brilliant. I was just a girl who'd been abandoned at every turn before being plucked out of her crappy old life. A girl who didn't belong in her old world and who didn't know how to fit into this new one. My throat felt thick and tight, and I blinked, once, twice, staring down at my boots.

And suddenly it wasn't just my boots in my line of vision. Taliok's long, dark, three-clawed feet were very close to mine. I jerked, looking up, realizing he'd stepped towards me. There was a breath of space between us, still, but that was it. If I took a really deep breath, my breasts would brush against his abs. I fought the insane urge to breathe in as much air as I could. Slowly, I looked up to meet Gahn Taliok's gaze. I froze at what I saw there. Thunderous darkness. His face was twisted in fury, his sight stars pulled to sharp, dense points.

Seeing the unhappiness in his face triggered a fight or flight response in me, as years of my parents' anger, and then my crappy ex's, resurfaced in my body. My heart thundered, and sweat poured. But Gahn Taliok's anger seemed different than what I was used to. And when he spoke next, I understood why – because it wasn't directed at me.

"I do not understand your expressions well," he muttered, his voice like broken steel. "But I fear I have bothered you again." His tail whipped back and forth on the sand behind him, and his jaws snapped miserably.

He doesn't blame me. The realization exploded inside me. *He doesn't blame me. He doesn't think I'm an evil child who needs saving like my parents did. And he doesn't think I'm too lazy, stupid, and weak to live without him like my ex did. He doesn't blame me for any of this.*

If anything, his unhappiness seemed directed at himself. Or maybe at the whole situation. For the first time, I felt a bit of sympathy for him. From what I understood, for the Sea Sand people, when the Lavrika showed them their mate, both people instantly felt a deep bond. To feel that for someone, and not have it reciprocated the way you'd expected, must have been agony.

And yet, he asked nothing of me. Even now, less than a step away from me, he didn't touch me. He'd mentioned the fact that he'd seen me as a vision of his mate. But so far, he hadn't asked me to actually... do anything.

His words hung in the air between us, heavy like the stone I'd been examining just a few moments before.

"You didn't bother me," I finally whispered. His sight stars pulsed at my response.

"You look unhappy," he said. When I took my next deep breath, my breasts actually did brush against him, sending a shocking spark between my legs. Taliok's sight stars exploded, and his tail jerked on the sand, but he made no other move. *I should step back. I should move away from him...*

But I didn't.

"You didn't make me unhappy. It's... complicated."

"Tell me the ways it is complicated," he growled. "And I will make it simple."

Gahn Taliok's voice was firm, very sure, but gentle at the same time. It caressed my skin, and I closed my eyes for the briefest moment against the sound. When I opened them again, it was to the sight of those same black and gold eyes, boring into mine. And before I could stop myself, words were tumbling out of my mouth.

"What you said before. About me being brilliant. Or brilliance. I'm not used to people saying things like that about me. And I don't trust it."

He tilted his head slightly, making his scarred, bent ear look even lower than the other one.

"You do not trust my words?" he asked, seeming genuinely confused. "Why?"

"Because every time someone I cared about has said something nice to me," I explained, "it's been to get something. It's been to control me or manipulate me. It wasn't honest."

Gahn Taliok's fingers stretched at his sides.

"Then it is as I thought," he said. "It is simple. These people you speak of did not deserve you. They were fools. Or they were blind." He paused and then bent incrementally lower. "I may be a fool, and some may say I'm blind. But I would never deceive you. And in this, I know I am not wrong."

It was hard to breathe. My eyes were burning. I barely got my next words out.

"How can I trust you? I don't even know you."

"It is my greatest wish that you would know me." His voice sounded reverent, almost fevered. "These ones who've lied to you, I know they did not deserve you. I do not yet know if I deserve you. But I will spend every day of my life striving to be worthy of you."

His nostrils flared, and his face got closer yet again. I tipped my head back to keep my eyes locked on his. Maybe if I just looked deep enough, stared hard enough, I could see if he was telling the truth. To see if he really meant to hurt me in the end.

This close, I could see just how deep his scars went. And as if someone had taken possession of my damn hand, I suddenly reached out. Without even knowing what I was doing, I traced my fingertips over the shredded bend of his ear, down over his scarred brow, all the way down to his hard, mangled jaw. He stiffened under my touch, his body turning to stone. But his skin was so warm.

He was so fucking tense. His muscles bulging and clenching.

Maybe he doesn't want me to touch him. Hell, I don't even know why I'm doing this...

"Is this alright?" I breathed. My gaze roamed over him, settling in fascination on his carved abdomen as he drew in quick, shallow breaths.

"Yes," he choked out. My heart rocketed up to my throat, and I ran my fingers lower, down his neck, to the deep, grey, ragged lines on his chest. I knew this was crazy, this was fucking insane, but I couldn't stop myself. It was like I'd been hypnotized, my hand drawn like a magnet to his skin.

But when my hand moved lower, down his abs, and his pelvis jerked, I realized why he was so goddamned tense. His loincloth was pulled forward and tight against the power of a massive erection.

Like I'd been burned, I yanked my hand back.

What the hell has gotten into you? I thought angrily. *You're going to give him false hope.*

But was it false hope? Because even though I'd taken my hand away, all I wanted to do was reach out and touch him again. And it kind of terrified me.

"I... I should get back to work," I stammered. "You know. My rocks."

I stepped away quickly. Too quickly, it turned out. I ended up stepping on the rock I'd tossed down, and my knee buckled as my ankle gave out. So fast it was like lightning, like a fucking bullet, Gahn Taliok's hand shot out and grabbed my wrist to stop me from falling. But clearly, he wasn't prepared for how his natural strength measured up against my human frame, and as he pulled, I collided with him.

It was like running into a boulder. Thick, powerful, and unforgiving. I gasped. Those same words could be applied to Gahn Taliok's cock, pressing into my stomach through my solar protection jacket.

Heat bloomed in my belly, shooting out everywhere. Into every limb, and pulsing between my legs.

Did these guys have some kind of alien magic I didn't know about? Why did this guy have such an effect on me? First, he had me spilling my guts in a way I hadn't done with anyone else. And now I was getting aroused, just from the feel of his hard body against mine.

This was bad. So, so bad.

I'd thought my walls were strong. Untouchable, even.

But there was Gahn Taliok, standing on the other side with a chisel, chipping and chipping away.

And, if I wasn't careful, that chisel could turn into a fucking wrecking ball.

8
TALIOK

elanie crashed against my chest with a soft little *oof* sound. My hand tightened against her wrist, now crushed between us, and my other hand shot up to steady her instinctively. It settled on her lower back. My breath came ragged, my chest heaving. My cock strained insistently. This was a desire unlike anything I'd ever known. More than hunger. More than thirst. More than the need to breathe. The weight of the feeling almost crushed me. The feeling of holding the entire world in my arms.

Before I could stop myself, my head had lowered against the strange fabric of her hood. I huffed in a huge breath, letting the scent of her penetrate. My cock surged against her body. My instinct, the fever of my body, demanded that I push her to the sands and rut her. Right now. But, though next to her delicate beauty I may have looked a beast, I would not act like one.

"Gahn Taliok," she whispered against my chest.

"Do not call me Gahn. Never Gahn. Not you," I said against her hood, fighting to keep my strained voice from sounding like a snarl. It was strange having my people call me Gahn, but I was starting to get used to it. But having Melanie call me such a thing was all wrong. I would raise my tail before her and call her Gahnala every day for the rest of our lives. But I was not Gahn. Not to her. She had all the power, here.

So when she began to pull away, muttering that she should get back to her rocks, I let her go. Having her step out of my embrace was a wound.

But it was only one of many. And I'd healed from every other wound before. My scars were proof.

Her face, in the shadow of her hood, was stained strangely pink. She was panting, too, and I worried that something was wrong. But she seemed to be well enough when she turned her attention back towards the cliff, crouching to examine a small pebble on the sand. She looked so lovely and focused. It made me want to give her things. But what? What could I possibly offer her?

Then it hit me.

"You should come to my people's mountains. We have many more types of stones there."

Her head whipped around.

"Really?"

My tail swished in eagerness.

"Yes, more kinds than I can count," I answered. I would bring her every stone on this planet if it made her happy. I'd build a throne of them, a whole world of them.

"Hmm, that might be good," she said. "Kat and I have been looking for certain minerals to make more of the *sunscreen* the humans need. But we haven't had any luck."

I stared, not willing to speak, not even willing to breathe, in case it made her change her mind. *Please, let me give you this,* I thought silently. *Let me give you everything.*

But that flash of interest was gone.

"Let me think about it," she said, closing down. I stared

73

down at her as she continued her work. I wanted to say so much. But I did not have the words. There were no words for this. This ache.

I could have remained there, watching her, forever. But my good ear pricked at the sound of someone approaching. I turned, instinctively putting my body between Melanie and whoever was coming. It was Oxriel, my warrior.

He raised his tail. When it lowered, I saw his eyes shift to Melanie, crouching in the sand, before returning to me.

"Exoka wishes to see you," he said.

Exoka. The Gahnala of our tribe.

Fol-Gahnala, I corrected myself. Now that her mate, Gahn Irokai, had died, she was the Fol-Gahnala. The current Gahnala of our tribe, Melanie, was not officially Gahnala yet. Not until she accepted me as mate, and we performed the Gahnala-Kai. My heart surged at the thought, and my cock throbbed. But I had to focus. The moment between Melanie and me had passed, and I had other duties to attend to.

I cast one last look down at Melanie. But she was too absorbed now in her work to watch me go. Not wishing to distract her further, I turned and began to walk with Oxriel back towards our people's settlement. As I did, I heard soft words called after me. Whispering to me. Following me.

"See you later."

I forced myself to keep walking. To keep going. Because if I turned around now, I'd be trapped forever. I'd never leave Melanie's side again. And this would not make her happy.

Oxriel and I exited the main area of the settlement and walked along the cliffs, approaching the crack that led to our people's clearing.

"That new woman... Is she the one whose face you saw? In the Lavrika's pools?" Oxriel asked.

. . .

I TENSED FOR A MOMENT, though I was not sure why. Oxriel had no insulting tone to his voice. Nothing but respectful curiosity. It seemed I wanted to keep everything about Melanie to myself. But that was useless. Soon enough, all would know she was my mate. When she agreed to be my Gahnala.

If she agrees.

Miserably, I shoved that thought aside and answered Oxriel.

"Yes," I said.

He made a thoughtful sound, then fell silent as we entered our people's clearing.

The area had been transformed since yesterday. Where it had once been a large, empty circle surrounded by walls of rock, it was now filled with tents and people. Our tribe was not very large, only half the size of Gahn Fallo's, and some of my men had remained back in the mountains to guard our territory. But the place felt alive with movement and people now. The only thing missing was Melanie, back with her fellow women, so brutally far from me.

"Where has the Fol-Gahnala made her home?" I asked Oxriel, scanning the various dakrival hide tents that had been erected.

"There," Oxriel said, gesturing with his tail towards a large tent near the back of the clearing, against the cliff wall. I grunted, snapping my tail in thanks, and went towards it.

When I reached the tent I stopped, calling inside.

"Fol-Gahnala. It is me. It is Taliok."

"Don't you mean *Gahn* Taliok?" a familiar voice called. "Come in."

That voice was warmth in my chest. I pulled the tent's flap aside and stepped in.

The Fol-Gahnala Exoka's tent looked just as it had when she'd shared it with Gahn Irokai, back in the mountains.

75

And I would know, as I had lived there for a time as a boy. The only difference now was that most of Gahn Irokai's weapons had been dispersed among the warriors of our tribe, and there was only a single blade left by the bed of hides.

"You are the second woman I have told today not to call me Gahn," I muttered, my words to Melanie earlier echoing in my head.

The Fol-Gahnala turned towards me from where she'd been lighting a valok candle. She placed the candle on a tray of bone on the ground by the bed. Its flickering light illuminated her features. She was a fair bit younger than Gahn Irokai had been. Where Gahn Irokai's braid had been all grey at the time of his death, Exoka's was only slightly streaked. But I couldn't help but notice how many more streaks there were since her mate had died. And how many new lines had formed around her eyes and mouth.

"And who was the first?" she asked. Like I had with Oxriel, I found myself pausing. But there was nothing to hide from Exoka. The woman had treated me like her own son alongside her daughters, Lakai and Roxala, after my parents had died.

"My mate. Melanie." It felt good to say her name. Good in the way cleansing a wound felt good. A sting that made me catch my breath.

"This is wise," Exoka said, a smile tilting her mouth upwards. "A man would have to be a fool indeed to make his mate call him Gahn. And I know you are no fool."

I grunted, and sat heavily on the sand, cross-legged.

"I am not so sure," I muttered, running a claw absent-mindedly through the sand.

"Why do you say that, Taliok?"

She sat down across from me, settling her hands on her knees.

"My mate does not feel the sacred mate bond. I am trying to win her to me. But it is... difficult."

Exoka regarded me thoughtfully.

"I do not have advice for you, Taliok. The sacred mate bond was strong and swift in me with Irokai." She paused then, smiling softly, her eyes glinting. "It is no secret that Irokai and I would have liked to see you mated to Lakai or Roxala. If the Lavrika had chosen a woman of the Sea Sands for you, you would not be dealing with this. But now, Lakai and Roxala have their own families. And you will have to build yours."

She was right. If my mate was a woman from our people, she would feel the sacred mate bond immediately, as I did. But I was glad that I had not been joined with Lakai or Roxala. I cared for them, but I considered them sisters. And now that I knew Melanie, with all her serious softness, I could not imagine loving anyone else this way.

Exoka's voice broke me me out of my thoughts.

"I have never known you to shy away from something difficult, Taliok. There are few as determined or as strong as you. Not many men would have been able to do what you did for your father and you were all of a child, then."

She was referring to the day my father had died, of course. The day I'd gotten my scars. I did not answer.

She spoke again.

"I have no doubt that you will conquer anything you put the blade of your will to."

It was a typical motherly response. One of pure love and faith. I had no doubt she believed it. But it had no true bearing in reality. Her support was kind. But it was ultimately meaningless. Melanie was not a battle to be won, or a krixel to be killed. She was not something to be conquered. If anything, she had conquered me. I was powerless against her.

With a jerk of my tail, I changed the subject.

"I have to apologize, Fol-Gahnala," I said.

Her tail swiped dismissively.

"Just as you ask me not to call you Gahn, I will ask you not call me Fol-Gahnala, Taliok. And what are you apologizing for?"

Bitter rage set my teeth on edge.

"For not killing the filthy Fallo."

Exoka flinched, then looked away, staring into the flame of the single candle beside us.

"I know your reasons for not doing so must have been good. I know you hungered for Gahn Fallo's blood even more than I," she said quietly.

"Gahn Buroudei and his mate demanded peace," I explained. "The new women will remain here only if blood is not shed. Otherwise, they will return to Fallo's hills."

Exoka's mouth hardened, and she turned back to me.

"Then you made the right choice, Taliok. You are wise, just as I have said. The new women bring new life, new chances, and hopefully new children to our tribes. Protecting that, protecting our future, is more important than the spilled blood of the past."

So she saw it as I did. It was good to hear. Now I knew my reasoning was sound, and that I hadn't forgone killing Fallo out of some selfish need to not drive away my mate.

When I said no more, Exoka shifted on the sand, turning and grabbing something nearby. When she laid it on the ground between us, I recognized what it was. Her Gahnala-Kai Rek. Long leather strips braided with the veroar vines of our mountains created a long net to fit along her tail. Ablik beads, along with beads made from other stones, stones found only in our mountains, gleamed in the candlelight. Deep red, shining orange, and cloudy grey.

She ran her hands down the length of the beaded

garment, her sight stars like mist. Like she was looking into the past.

"I still remember when Irokai wound this up my tail." She paused, then drew a heavy breath. "It is why I have called you here, Taliok."

Her claws sprang into quick motion, unbraiding one long strip of the Gahnala-Kai Rek. In a moment, she'd freed the largest bead: a round, shimmering grey stone half the size of my thumb.

"Agrippar stone," I said, holding out my hand as she passed it to me.

"Yes," the Fol-Gahnala said. "Irokai collected every one of these stones himself. You will do the same for your Gahnala. But you will add this one. Irokai would have wanted you to have it."

My chest ached. Gahn Irokai had been a second father to me, and Exoka a second mother. To have him gone was a terrible pain. And to see her without him was even worse.

I turned my gaze downward to the smooth stone in my hand. It wasn't a clear stone. And it wasn't opaque. It was somewhere in between. Cloudy. Unwilling to yield its secrets. Demanding study.

Just like my mate.

"This is a great gift," I said. "Thank you."

Exoka's tail swished and we met gazes once more before she stood and led me to her tent's flap.

"Leave me for now, Taliok. I have other things to do this day and night."

I raised my tail in acknowledgement, then slipped out. The stone smooth and heavy in my hand, I began to walk towards my tent.

My empty tent.

The tent where I would sit, alone, and dream of a quiet woman from beyond the stars.

9
MELANIE

"Find anything cool today?"

Kat was lying in her bed of hides, on her stomach, her head turned towards me as she spoke. Her hands were folded under her chin. I shimmied out of my pants and shirt, laying them next to my hides for tomorrow. All around us, the other women were undressing and getting ready to sleep for the night.

"No. Nothing for the sunscreen project, anyway," I replied.

"Damn," she said before yawning, her mouth opening wide like a cat's. "I wonder if something like zinc oxide just doesn't exist here. Maybe we need to switch focus. Maybe look at the plants..."

I sat on my hides in my bra and underwear, before lying down, too.

I chewed the inside of my lip, wondering if I should tell Kat what Taliok had suggested to me earlier. About going to his mountains.

I may as well. Then Kat can talk some sense into me about why going there would be a very bad idea.

"Gahn Taliok said he'd take me to his people's mountains," I said in a rush. "He said there are a lot more types of rocks and minerals there."

Kat's eyes, which had been far away as she'd pondered, snapped to mine. She sat up, her wiry frame in her underwear a total contrast to my thick curves.

"For real? That sounds amazing!" she exclaimed.

"What?" I watched her in confusion for a moment. Kat was one of the biggest advocates for *not* going off with an alien. I couldn't believe she thought it was a good idea. "Why is that amazing?"

"Because this planet is unreal, and I'd love to see more of it!" she said excitedly. "Before this, I'd never been outside Detroit. I've never seen fucking mountains, man. That's wild. Plus it would be great to see what other natural materials exist on this planet. They might be useful for lots of things." She paused, then said, "If you don't want to go, do you think Gahn Taliok would take me?"

I had been counting on Kat to tell me I couldn't go, to talk me down from whatever weird ledge I'd found myself on. I was not prepared for this reaction. And I was even less prepared for the barb of jealousy, deep in my gut, and the thought of Gahn Taliok taking someone else to his mountains instead of me.

Oh, God. Jealousy? Really? Where is this coming from?

Kat narrowed her blue eyes, tipping her head.

"Well you can't go alone," I said quickly. "If you want to go, I'll go, too. So it's safer."

See? I'm not jealous. I'm just looking out for my friend. Buddy system and all that.

Kat grinned, then snuggled back down into her hides.

"Sick. Can we go tomorrow?"

Tomorrow? A days-long journey with Taliok, starting tomorrow? That felt way too soon.

"I'll find out," I said noncommittally. It looked like I was locked in now.

"Y'all good with lights out?"

Theresa was holding the last lit candle in the tent. A chorus of "yeah" and "OK" and "goodnight" went through the group, and she blew it out, plunging the tent into darkness. I didn't feel like I could sleep yet, though. A bundle of nerves had settled into a knot in my belly. Nerves and, strangely, excitement. No, I couldn't deny it. I was actually kind of excited about the idea of going to the mountains. Was I excited, like Kat was, for the trip itself and what we could learn? Or was I excited for who would be taking us?

Ugh. That was a question I was not prepared to answer.

I laid awake for a long time, trying to force myself to sleep. But it didn't work. And because of that, I was awake to hear the alien call of my name from outside the tent.

I sat up, clutching the hides to my chest, straining my ears. I flinched when the sound came again.

"Gahnala Melanie."

It was an alien woman's voice.

Not Taliok.

Hold on. Was that disappointment?

Just get dressed.

I slipped back into my clothing as quietly as possible, not bothering with socks, boots, or my jacket. Then I went to the flap of the tent, lifting it slightly and looking out.

All of the alien women I'd met so far were tall and beautiful in their own alien way. But the woman standing before me was truly impressive. She was taller than many other women, and her long dark hair was streaked with silver that shone under the stars. When she raised her tail over her eyes, I saw that it was decorated with an intricately beaded garment.

82

What had Bokɜelie called that? A Gahnala-Kai Rek. She's a Gahnala. A queen.

Of course. She must be the Gahnala of the third tribe.

I stepped quickly out of the tent and without even thinking about it, gave a little bow. It probably looked fucking stupid, but I had no idea what else to do. I didn't have a tail to raise in respect, and it felt laughable that this elegant alien queen was raising her tail for *me.* Just quiet, human me.

When I straightened, the woman pinned me with two large, intelligent eyes.

"You are Gahnala Melanie?" she asked.

"Just Melanie," I said with a nod.

Her mouth twitched into a slight smile.

"It is good to meet you, just Melanie. I am the Fol-Gahnala Exoka. I wish to have your company for a time if that is agreeable."

"It is," I said slowly, and slightly warily. What could an alien queen, the Fol-Gahnala of Taliok's tribe want with me? Unless...

"Are you Gahn Taliok's mother?" The question was out of my mouth before I could consider if it was a rude one. But she smiled again and didn't seem offended. I was glad she wasn't, because I was curious. I wasn't too sure how the Gahns were chosen, yet. It made sense that it could be something like human royalty, where it was passed down through lineage.

"I am not Taliok's mother. Though I have been like one to him since his own mother died. And my fallen mate, Gahn Irokai, was like a father to him."

We began walking. It felt natural to do so while talking. There was no one else out at this hour, aside from whatever patrolling or hunting parties may have been out on the sands. Other than that, everyone was in their tents for the night.

"I'm sorry," I said, thinking of her husband, remembering that Gahn Fallo had killed him in the big battle.

I felt Exoka's eyes on me from the side.

"Have you done something wrong? Why do you apologize?"

"Oh. I guess it's a human thing," I replied. "When someone dies, we often say, 'I'm sorry,' to their family and friends."

We left the main settlement area and walked along the cliffs on the sand. It felt cool on my bare feet, unlike the heat of the day.

"Ah," Exoka said. "The people of the Sea Sands do not say sorry for these things. They take revenge."

Goosebumps erupted over my skin. The night felt suddenly colder. Exoka kept speaking.

"Taliok would have avenged Irokai. But he did not. And now, he will not."

I let out a small breath. I didn't personally like Gahn Fallo all that much, but I didn't want to see him get killed, especially now that Chapman was his mate. The less violence, the better.

But if revenge is so important for their people... why...?

"Why not? Why won't Taliok do it?"

I couldn't help but ask. I was too curious. It didn't make sense.

We stopped in front of a large crevice in the cliffs. Exoka fixed her eyes on me.

"Why not? Because of you, of course."

I stared at her, not understanding.

Exoka's face softened into a wan smile.

"Taliok knows that by killing Gahn Fallo, he will destroy the peace here and he will lose you," she explained in a quiet voice.

I had no fucking clue what to say to that. To know that I was the reason Taliok hadn't done something that important to his loved ones and their culture, something that important for his grief was... A lot. I felt like I needed to say sorry all over again, and was opening my mouth to do just that when Exoka spoke.

"Do not trouble yourself over it. It was the correct decision. Taliok is a wise Gahn."

I nodded, absorbing everything she'd said. We started walking again, moving into the crevice, which soon opened up into a deep clearing area, surrounded by the walls of the cliffs. The space was dotted with tents. *Their settlement.* My eyes scanned the tents, looking for Taliok. When I realized what I was doing, I forced myself to stop. *Why are you looking around for him like some girl with a secret crush?*

I focused my attention back to Exoka. I had a feeling it wasn't every day the Fol-Gahnala of the newly killed Gahn came to seek you out. And curiosity was burning a hole through my stomach, knowing now that she was as close a living person to a mother that Taliok had.

"Is it alright if I ask..." I began. "What happened to Taliok's parents? And how did he become Gahn if it's not based on lineage?"

We came to a stop outside a large tent on the far edge of the settlement near the cliff wall. Exoka's shoulders seemed to fall slightly and she turned to face me. The lines of her face looked deeper.

"Taliok's mother died not long after he was born. And then, when he was just a young boy, out on a hunting trip with his father, a krixel attacked."

I shuddered at the mention of the krixel. I'd never seen one, but Theresa and Chapman had, and their description of the man-sized, clawed, bat monster had been horrifying.

"The krixel killed Taliok's father," Exoka continued. "Even

85

as a child, Taliok was strong. Very strong. He killed the krix-el." She stopped, her jaw churning, as if the next part was hard to get out.

"Taliok waited at his father's side for a full day and a full night, hoping he would wake. When he did not, Taliok dragged his father's body back to our people's tents. This took another three full days and nights. It is why he has such deep scars. His wounds began to close without the aid of Lavrika's blood, and they healed badly."

Horror swept through me, and my throat tightened up. The thought of Gahn Taliok, tiny and young, sitting next to the body of his father, alone out on the sands, made me want to fucking weep. And then thinking of him, torn open and bleeding, pulling his father home...

Holy shit.

There was a hell of a lot I didn't know about this guy. But if what Exoka had said was true, then he had a deep strength to him that, even among these alien warriors, was unparal-leled. It had to be. Because that wasn't just strength of the body. But of the mind. The heart. Strength of character. And it made me want to know more. More about the quiet, brooding, scarred man whose eyes were like shattered gold. The one who already felt so much for me.

Exoka took a few breaths, as if that part of the story had taken a lot of energy from her.

"After Taliok's father's death, Irokai and I took him into our tent and raised him alongside our daughters. When Irokai died in battle, he named Taliok Gahn. It was his dying wish."

Her voice became strained on those last words. Now that I knew saying "I'm sorry" didn't mean much to her, I wasn't sure what else to say. Instead, I reached a tentative hand forward and gently gripped her forearm. Her sight stars pulsed as if surprised, but then she smiled.

"Taliok is a good man," she said softly. "Very strong. But he is not proud. I will not try to sway your feelings, but I will say that I do not believe there is a better man among our people."

She patted my hand, then turned to the tent, lifting the flap and stepping inside.

"Thank you for speaking with me, Melanie. Taliok will walk you back to your people. It is not safe for you to go alone."

The tent flap fell closed before I could ask where Gahn Taliok was, or how to find him. But an invisible whisper of sensation lit up my spine, and everything in me clenched.

I whirled around.

And there he was.

Silent and dark, he watched me. I took a step closer, taking in his form. The moonlight turned him into carved marble. I couldn't deny that he was beautiful. He was. The black and gold eyes that followed me everywhere. The broad face and hard jaw. The body that looked like a god's. Even the more alien, kangaroo features were graceful on him. And the scars didn't detract from the image, either. They were a sign of his strength.

Such strength... I couldn't imagine being through what he'd been through. I'd been through some shit, for sure. But he had experienced something few ever would.

Exoka's words echoed.

He dragged his father's body back to our tents. This took another three full days and nights...

Tears sprang to my eyes. I couldn't stop them. And I couldn't stop myself from taking another step forward and sweeping his hands into mine.

He jerked as if I'd branded him even though all I was doing was holding his huge, clawed hands. I stared down at his hands in mine, trying to imagine them smaller, pulling his father all the way home. The image was a fucking tragic one. It broke my heart. I sniffed, and a huge tear fell from my eye right onto his palm.

And then I was crushed against him, his arms like bars of iron around me, pulling me into his broad, scarred chest. His hands moved frantically up and down my back, then to my neck, finally settling on either side of my jaw, tilting my face up to look at his. His eyes looked feral, his fangs bared.

"I have heard tell of this," he snarled. "Of this human crying. Tell me who has hurt you. Tell me now, and I will end them."

I knew without the slimmest shadow of a doubt that he meant it. He'd kill for me. And not just that. He'd *stop* himself from killing for me. He hadn't taken revenge against Gahn Fallo, for himself and his adoptive mother, because of what he felt for me.

What are the chances that this guy is the real fucking deal? Not someone who would hurt me, or abandon me, or try to control me?

I couldn't say for sure yet. But if I judged based on the frantic ferocity of his face alone, then yes, it would appear that Gahn Taliok was indeed the *real fucking deal.*

I sniffed again, then blinked a bunch of times, trying to force the tears to stop.

"I'm OK. I just... I heard something sad." Exoka hadn't told me the story was a secret, but I wasn't sure if I should mention the details or not.

"You heard something sad?" Taliok asked. "And you had such a strong reaction just from hearing it?"

I laughed at his earnest confusion, a short sad hiccup through the tears.

"Well, it was really, really sad," I replied.

His face bent lower, his nose almost touching mine. The hot fan of his breath over my skin made me shiver.

"You are too beautiful and good. Such a soft heart..."

He shifted slightly, his nose bumping my forehead. He tensed, then inhaled deeply against my hair. My heart hammered, a frenzy in my chest that echoed between my legs. His body was so hard and warm. His hands were like goddamn steel, but somehow tender.

This is crazy. This is absolutely crazy. You need to stop this. You need to run. You need to protect yourself.

Hadn't I been the one shocked at Cece and Chapman's easy trust in their mates? And yet here I suddenly was, tipping my head further back, rising up on my tippy toes so I could try to brush my lips against Gahn Taliok's.

Taliok. Not Gahn Taliok. He told you not to call him Gahn.

Taliok's hands moved down. I had never been petite, but those massive alien hands almost completely encircled my plushly curved waist. When I reached up to splay my hands on his muscled chest, pressing into the warmth of his skin, his fingers clenched against my flesh and he shuddered. He pulled me tighter against him, against the whole length of him. Against his thick, stiff cock. He groaned, a brutal animal sound against my skin. I felt that groan in every part of my body. My nipples hardened. My breath caught in my throat as I parted my lips.

10

TALIOK

I had never been this close to Melanie for so long. Her softness under my claws was a supple agony. I had to restrain myself from holding her as tightly as possible. It would crush her.

But it was hard not to. There was too much in me. Too much. Too much love choking in my chest. Too much blood in my cock. It was intoxicating. Unrelenting. It made me want to pull her down to the sands, climb atop her, and press into her. Every instinct in my body was driving me to do it. But I couldn't. She did not yet feel the mate bond for me. And even if she did, how did one get from here to there? From holding each other to mating?

Maybe she will tell me when she is ready. Melanie's mouth was open slightly, but she was not saying anything. And since she was not currently ripping her clothes off and jumping, naked, upon my cock, I could only surmise that she did not want to mate.

Pull back, Taliok. Pull back now.

"It is late. We should return to your tent," I said.

Unless you want to come to mine. Those words remained unspoken, and Melanie's mouth clamped shut.

"Oh. OK. You're right."

Reluctantly, I let my arms fall away from the soft allure of her body. She rubbed her hands up and down over her arms, quickly.

"Why do you do that?" I asked her.

"I have *goosebumps*," she said. We walked side by side, out of my tribe's settlement towards the exit from the cliffs.

"What are *goosebumps*?" I watched her from the side of my eyes, being careful not to stare. Though it was difficult. For she shone more than all our broken moons.

"It happens to human skin when we're cold. Or other times..."

"You are cold?" I jerked to look at her, fully staring now. I could not help it. I had never heard of an adult being cold. The only ones who were ever at risk of becoming cold were newborn infants at night. The humans were so vulnerable. The thought scared me. *How do I make her warm?* I had no hides or clothing with me besides my loincloth. I was reaching to undo it so that I could toss it around her shoulders when she spoke again.

"I'm actually not cold." She turned her head up to me, a slight quirk on her mouth. "This is one of those other times."

I grunted, wondering what the "other times" were. But Melanie said no more, and I was not sure if I should ask.

We had reached the open sands. I jogged around Melanie so she was closer to the cliff, repositioning myself so that if any threat came from the sands, it would reach me before her. We made our way along the cliff face in silence. I thought of Zeezee's advice to talk to Melanie. *Is this when I should talk to her? But what should I say?*

Melanie saved me from coming up with something to talk about.

"I've decided to go to the mountains with you. My friend Kat wants to come, too."

My heart leapt. The thought of Melanie in the lands of my people was a stirring one. And deeply arousing. I reached down and adjusted my still-hard cock.

"This is good," I said, meaning it. Getting Melanie away from the other tribes, showing her my homeland... It was very, very good. "When do you want to go?"

Let us go now, I thought to myself. *As soon as possible. Leave by the light of the stars and never look back.*

"Well, Kat wants to go tomorrow," Melanie replied.

Tomorrow.

It is not now, but it is the next best thing.

"That is agreeable. We can leave in the morning."

We walked together into the large settlement, past Buroudei's people's tents, then in towards the centre, to the human tent.

We stopped just outside the tent, facing each other. Melanie's eyes looked deep and dark in the night air.

"Thanks for walking me back. I guess I'll see you tomorrow."

My tail swished behind me in agreement. Tomorrow already seemed too far away.

Melanie moved to go inside, grabbing a hold of the tent flap and pulling it back before hesitating. She let it fall, then turned and took two quick steps until she was standing before me. My cock ached at her nearness. My breath came ragged. *She is torturing me. Why?*

"Bend down," she said. Her words were quiet. A whisper on the night air.

Confused, but willing to obey any order my Gahnala gave, I did so, bending towards her.

"Lower," she whispered. I did so until my face was level with hers. Her eyes searched mine. My hands shook at my sides as I restrained them from reaching for her.

But that restraint was folly. It was for nothing. Because when Melanie suddenly leaned forward, her soft, small lips pressing against mine, I could not stop myself from touching her. The soft slick of her lips over mine was dizzying, and my hands caught her delicate jaw before sliding back through her long dark hair. She gave a small gasp, and that sound exploded under my skin, making every muscle clench. When her lips parted, instinctively I pressed my tongues forward, inward, to taste her. Her one wide, wet tongue met mine, running along the length of my longest, central tongue. The sensation was exquisite. Though it was not mating, any part of me being inside any part of her was perfection. *I will never find pleasure like this again in my whole life. I could search the sands forever, and never find a joy like this.*

Melanie pulled back, planting a final soft press of her lips against my mouth. She panted, staring up at me, her mouth shining and wet. That wetness was a vision of erotic beauty unlike any other. It made me want to sink my cock into it. But her mouth was so small. She would never be able to take it, I was sure.

But I was getting ahead of myself. Because she was already pulling away and was making no mention of doing anything with my fat and heavy cock.

"Goodnight, Taliok," she whispered, stepping back. Her hands trailed down my chest and then fell to her sides, leaving echoes of fire in their wake.

I could not choke out a greeting in return. I made a strangled grunting sound and watched hungrily as she slipped into the darkness of the tent.

Can a man die from an untouched cock?

As her absence overwhelmed me, I felt that I could die. I knew men could die from blood loss. What about if all your blood was pulsing in your groin? The lack of it in my head made me feel slow and stupid. Like a beast whose only thought was of rutting.

But a beast was no good for Melanie. She was intelligent and beautiful and soft-hearted. I would have to strive, every day, to be a better man for her. I would work, every moment, so that I might taste her mouth again.

I was not sure why she had opened her mouth to me in the first place. But I was grateful.

And I would do everything in my power to make sure that it happened again.

11

MELANIE

The sound of the other girls rising, dressing, and chatting around me woke me in the morning. I sat up slowly, rubbing my eyes and squinting in the bright sunlight that filtered in through the gaps in the tent's walls. *I'm so groggy...*

It all came tumbling back. I was extra tired because I'd been out later than normal with Taliok. I'd told him we'd go with him to the mountains today. And I'd kissed him

I drew my knees up to my chest, resting my forehead against them. Why? Why had I done that? Why had I made such a move, and probably given him some kind of false hope? I wasn't ready to be his mate, right? So then why?

The image of him, looking so broken but beautiful and strong under the moonlight crashed in my brain, and I gasped, trying to muffle the sound so no one else would hear it. There was no escaping it. I'd kissed him because I'd wanted to. Because I'd wanted to get closer to him.

Stupid. Stupid stupid stupid.

And now I was about to go on a days-long journey with him alone?

Well, I wouldn't be alone. Kat yawned loudly as she rolled over beside me. She stretched languorously, then opened her large blue eyes.

"Morning," she said, sitting up.

"Morning. You still wanna go to the mountains?"

I ignored the fact that there was a part of me that almost hoped she'd say no. So that I would be alone with Taliok after all. *Stupid.*

"No shit, for real? Hell yes, I am! When are we going?" she asked.

"Today," I said, rising from my hides. "This morning, if you can be ready."

"You bet I can. Not like I have a whole suitcase of shit to pack." Kat grabbed one of the backpacks from the ship, then tossed in some spare uniform pants and tops. Gahn Fallo's men had gone back to the ship a little while ago and brought us a bunch of extra clothing and boots. Luckily the people of the Sea Sands had their own version of laundry, using a mixture of some of the cactus soap stuff with sand to scrub at any dirty clothing. After it was scrubbed, it was left out in the sun to dry and help kill off any bacteria and odour, and it left the hides, and our clothing, surprisingly soft and fresh-smelling. But it was still good to have extras. Especially underwear, which, thankfully, was included in the boxes with the uniforms. I joined Kat, packing extra clothes for myself in a bag, along with sunglasses, sunscreen, and extra socks. We both shrugged into our solar protection jackets, and before I knew it we were ready.

"Did I hear y'all say you're going to the mountains?"

Theresa was watching us as she put on her own jacket.

Kat nodded eagerly.

"We're running low on sunscreen. Geo Girl over here is gonna find some rocks then give 'em to me so I can whip something up." Kat's enthusiasm was infectious, and I found myself smiling at her explanation.

"Sounds good. Just… Be careful." Theresa's sunny face faltered. I reached out and squeezed her hand. Ever since she'd been cornered by a krixel in the cliffs in Gahn Fallo's territory, she'd been extra cautious about the flora and fauna here. Which was probably a good thing, considering half the flora and fauna on this damn planet could kill us. *Probably more than half of it, honestly.*

"We will be," I said, giving one last squeeze before letting go of her hand.

"Yeah, yeah, we'll be fine. Let's go!" Kat said. She had laced up her boots. I quickly did mine, and we headed for the tent's flap, lifting it and stepping out into the harsh sunlight.

I rummaged in my bag and put my sunglasses on immediately. So did Kat. Once on, I was able to stop squinting so much and actually open my eyes a little.

Only to see Taliok sitting on the sand, only a few paces from me. Heat flooded through me at the sight of him. He stood, graceful and quiet, and I gulped. The bright light of day laid open everything I'd done last night. But strangely, the night hadn't made my desires stronger. It wasn't like, now that it was morning, I didn't want to be around him. In fact, it scared me how much my body reacted to seeing him before my mind caught up. It was a jolt of what felt like… Joy.

"How long have you been here?" I asked, hefting my bag and walking up to Taliok.

"Since before the sun rose."

"Damn, son, you must be ready to hit the road, then!" Kat said, grinning widely under her dark sunglasses. I jumped at her voice. I'd completely forgotten she was there. When I saw Taliok, it was like he was the only thing that existed. I shook my head, hard. That was unlike me. I was always aware of my surroundings. Observant to a fault.

"What is a *road*?" Taliok asked, shifting his attention to Kat, frowning.

"It means you're ready to go. Hit the road, Jack, and don't you come back!"

The way Taliok's brow furrowed as he tried to understand Kat's random burst into English song was honestly adorable. I bit my lip, suppressing a broad smile.

"She's trying to say that we're ready if you are," I explained.

The swing of Taliok's golden eyes back to me was a visceral sensation. I felt a twinge, low in my body, when our eyes met. He held my gaze for a long moment, then breathed out, "Good."

Taliok bent and gathered some things that I hadn't noticed on the ground beside him. Two large leather-looking things, along with other leather bundles and collections of long dakrival bones.

"What's all that?" I asked.

"Saddles. We use them to teach our cubs to ride irkdu. I re-fashioned two from our tribe to fit you two better."

Oh, that was a relief. The only other time I'd ridden an irkdu was when Gahn Fallo's men had taken us to his territory for the first time after the zeelk attack. It had been brutal, and my thighs and gotten all torn up. We hadn't even ridden irkdu to move here, to the Cliffs of Uruzai. Instead, a large bone and hide sled had been built for the human women, and we'd been dragged here, along with the tents and supplies.

Taliok gestured to the other bundles.

"Food and valok. And materials for tents."

I nodded, my gaze lingering on the saddles. The fact he'd known to bring those for us was incredibly thoughtful.

"Sounds like we're set. We've got all our human shit too. Giddy up, let's roll," Kat said.

Taliok lifted the two saddles up onto one shoulder and carried the leather and bone bundles under his other arm.

"We must walk back towards my people's settlement. My irkdu is grazing somewhere near there. When we get there, I will call it."

We fell into step, the three of us, heading out of the settlement. And we would have kept on going, except for the familiar voice of Gahn Fallo cutting through the air.

"What are you doing here, Taliok? And where do you think you are going with the new women?"

The three of us stopped, and Kat rolled her eyes.

"Fuck off, Fallo," she called in English, but he ignored her, stalking up to Taliok. Taliok dropped what he was holding and immediately placed himself between Fallo and us two humans. He left his weapons, including the huge, curved blade, strapped to his back. But I saw the tense bunching of his back and shoulder muscles beneath his weapons' straps. And I saw the way his fingers twitched at his sides.

"We are going back to my people's mountains," Taliok said.

His voice was firm, and there was a dangerous growl of warning under the words. That growl resonated deep in my belly. There was something attractive about it. *Focus. This could get dangerous. Now is not the time for stupid fantasies.*

The handles of Gahn Fallo's many weapons were visible above his shoulders and jutting out from his sides behind his back. I knew Taliok was fucking strong. But I really didn't want this to turn ugly. I didn't want Fallo to have any opportunity to use one of those terrible blades on Taliok. God, I was feeling protective of him. This was bad. I was getting in too deep.

"You will not leave this place with them. I will not allow

it." Gahn Fallo's red sight stars pulsed menacingly, but Taliok didn't budge even a fraction of an inch. He met Fallo's wild glare with one that was steady and firm. His voice, when he spoke, set my teeth on edge with its dark malice.

"Do not give me yet another reason to kill you, Fallo."

Fallo snarled, and in a blur, he unsheathed two huge blades. Without even turning around to look, Taliok's arm swept back and found me, shoving me backward. I caught Kat's arm as I stumbled, pulling her away from the scene.

No! Please no.

Taliok pulled out his giant scythe-like blade and held it before him with both hands, face like stone. He looked like some kind of alien grim reaper. I had no doubt he'd kill Gahn Fallo, now. If Fallo didn't kill him first.

Fallo gnashed his fangs and stalked back and forth, his dozens of long braids swishing as he swung his head threateningly. He grinned madly, then prepared to strike -

NO!

The word was so loud inside my head I almost thought I'd said it out loud. But then I realized another woman was screaming something.

"Fallo, put that down!"

Fallo froze. The words had struck him like lightning, every muscle tightening and arching in response to the sound. Chapman was running over the sands from Fallo's tent. And she looked fucking pissed.

"What do you think you're doing?" she said, planting herself in front of Fallo, hands on her hips. Taliok still held his weapon at the ready.

"I am stopping Taliok from taking these new women from here. He has no right."

Chapman turned to look past Taliok's hulking form at Kat and me.

My voice shook slightly as I spoke.

"He's taking us to the mountains. We need to check out the minerals there. We volunteered to go."

She gave a curt nod, then turned back to her unruly mate.

"Sounds like they want to go. So you have no right to stop them. Put your weapons away."

"But Taliok…!"

"Now," Chapman repeated, her voice falling low. Grunting, Fallo sheathed his blades, and I breathed out shakily, relief running through me.

"You can let go of my arm now," Kat whispered to me, wincing.

"Fuck. Sorry," I said, letting her go. I didn't realize how hard I'd been squeezing until she'd said something.

The interaction had caught some attention. People were watching us from all areas of the settlement, and Gahn Buroudei was sprinting over, followed by some of his warriors.

"Why have weapons been drawn?" Buroudei growled as he reached us, pinning Taliok with his gaze. Taliok was the only one still holding his blade. And to be honest, I was kind of glad. I wanted him to be safe, to have every protection possible against any sort of threat.

Chapman and Kat quickly filled Buroudei in. I remained silent, my eyes stuck on Taliok's muscled back and thick thighs. As if by watching him hard enough, I could keep something bad from happening to him

"Gahn Fallo has not acted well, here. But he has a point," Buroudei said slowly. "That woman is Gahn Taliok's mate, and he can take her anywhere he wishes. But the other woman is not."

Kat turned to me.

"What the fuck?" she hissed. I shook my head. I'd have to explain that to her later.

"Another warrior from another tribe should accompany them on their journey," Buroudei continued.

"Good," Gahn Fallo said. "Send one of my warriors. My man Vakal will go."

"How about *no*," Chapman said, whirling on him. "Stop trying to control everything. One of Gahn Buroudei's men can go."

I tensed in fear for Chapman at the flare of anger in Gahn Fallo's eyes. But finally, he grunted, bowing to her words. Which was, frankly, really fucking impressive on her part.

"She has totally hypnotized that motherfucker, I'm telling you. The power of human pussy," Kat said, shaking her head. The words stirred all kinds of images I shouldn't have been thinking about – Taliok on his back, eyes dark with desire, hypnotized by my...

"This is agreeable," Buroudei said, cutting off my thoughts. "One of my men will go." Buroudei turned to the group of his warriors who had followed him. Before he could even ask for a volunteer, a young-looking warrior, the tallest of the group, stepped forward quickly.

"I will go!"

The volunteer smiled, then hastily raised his tail in respect, as if he'd forgotten to do so in his rush. When he lowered it again, he turned that smile towards Kat.

"Great, now we'll have two of these weirdos with us," she said, watching him.

"It's probably a good idea, having one warrior per human. In case we run into any trouble out there," I responded. But Kat didn't seem to share my feelings. She huffed and crossed her arms.

"Yeah, yeah. Can we go now?"

The young warrior from Buroudei's tribe hurried forward to help Taliok with the saddles and bags. Taliok gave him a wary look, but slowly sheathed his weapon.

"We will see you upon your return. Be safe," Gahn Buroudei said. Gahn Fallo growled, saying nothing more, turning to follow Chapman who was striding away from the scene. I could hear her chastising him all the way back to their tent.

We continued walking the way we had been going before our interruption. I tried to get my heart rate and breathing under control. After that mess, my stress levels were sky-high. Taliok was silent next to me, but I could hear the other warrior chattering on the other side of Kat.

"My name is Galok. I am glad to accompany you."

"Look, my duce, this is a work trip. Melanie and I have shit to do. So don't be getting any ideas that this is some fun field trip."

I couldn't help but give a shaky snort at Kat's words. Wasn't she the one all pumped to go on this trip because she wanted to ooh and ah over the mountains? Seeing her become a grumpy taskmaster was kind of hilarious. A moment later, I felt her hand on my arm, and she drew me closer as we walked, whispering to me.

"So you want to tell me what the fuck is going on with you and Talick?"

My eyes flashed over to him. I saw his ears twitch, but otherwise, he didn't make any indication that he'd heard Kat's words.

"Nothing really. Apparently I'm supposed to be his mate. But nothing's been... Decided." My words came haltingly. Because I honestly wasn't sure what to say. Yeah, apparently I was Taliok's fated mate. But it's not like we were an item or anything.

But you kissed him...

Well... Kat didn't need to know about that part.

Before we fully left the main settlement, Galok made a

103

high sharp sound, and an irkdu came lumbering out from a nearby crack in the cliffs.

"This is my mount." He grinned and gestured proudly at the ugly centipede-like creature coming towards us. Its purple reptilian snout, black teeth, and many, many eyes were unnerving, but from what I'd seen the irkdu were exceptionally well-trained and had never shown any aggression to us humans. Thank goodness.

"Cool story, bro," Kat muttered. Galok cocked his head at her words. The irkdu trailed behind us as we headed towards Taliok's settlement.

"*Cool story, bro,*" Galok repeated. "These are words from your language, no? Please translate them for me. I wish to know what a *cool story, bro* is."

Kat laughed sharply at that and gave him some snarky, noncommittal reply. I tuned them out, every sense automatically reaching for Taliok. I listened for the sound of his feet on the sand, the swish of his tail, his steady breathing, as we got closer to his settlement. Though there was a little space between us, I practically felt his skin against my sleeve. The sensation was so real that it was driving me crazy. At one point, I shifted slightly closer as I walked, pretending to avoid stepping on a stone, and brushed my arm against his.

What are you doing? What are you doing?

At the other settlement, like Galok had done, Taliok called – a high, piercing sound on the air. As he did so, I couldn't stop myself from staring at the thick column of his throat. I wanted to run my fingertips down it and feel the pulse of his heart. I wanted to trace those vicious scars with my tongue...

Oh, fucking hell. I really was attracted to him. That much was certain. But was it becoming more than that? Because that's what truly scared me.

Taliok's huge creature soon joined our little group. The

two warriors gave low commands as the two irkdu circled each other suspiciously. But then the huge beasts seemed to relax, seeing their masters so calm with each other.

"Each man will ride with a woman. Melanie will ride with me," Taliok said. He said it so simply, as if it were fact. *Melanie will ride with me.* At one point I may have found such an assertion annoying, but in this moment, it gave me a small thrill. But it clearly didn't thrill Kat.

"Hold on. I know you're a Gahn and all that, but you don't get to make decisions for her like that. Melanie, who do you want to ride with?"

Maybe it would be a good idea to get some distance between us. I could ride with Galok and maybe relax and enjoy this trip a little. Take some time to get my head on straight...

But the thought of Kat, or anyone else, sitting close to Taliok on his mount was not a relaxing one. And before I knew it, I was saying,

"It's OK. I'll ride with him."

Kat's mouth puckered into a frown, but she nodded. And, I couldn't help but notice the beaming smile of pure joy coming from Galok when he realized she'd be on his mount with him.

"I will secure the saddle, then I will help you up," Galok said, still smiling. To which Kat vehemently claimed that she didn't need his help. Shaking my head, I turned from them.

Taliok was already securing my saddle to his mount. He worked quickly and quietly, his huge muscles bulging under the hot sun. For such a gigantic, body-builder-looking alien warrior, he could move with some serious grace. His clawed fingers flew, tightening straps and attaching our supplies to his mount. Then he stepped away, looking at our companions.

"I did not bring enough dried meat for you, Galok. I did not expect you."

"It is no great matter," Galok replied breezily. He fixed his gaze on Kat again, and, oh my fucking *God*, literally puffed out his chest. "I am a skilled hunter." He seemed to say those last words more to Kat than anyone else. But apparently, she didn't care, because she'd turned her back on him and was trying to scrabble up the side of the huge creature Galok had just put the saddle on.

"Let me help you, small one," Galok chuckled.

I stepped up to Taliok's irkdu, turning my gaze away, not wanting to see Galok get his head ripped off for his words.

"Will you try to mount my irkdu alone, the way your friend does?" Taliok's voice was deep and low as he moved in behind me. When had he gotten so fucking close? Goosebumps erupted over my skin. If I leaned back even a fraction of an inch, I'd be pressed into Taliok's broad chest. I ignored that magnetic pull and answered him.

"No. Unlike Kat, I don't have any illusions about my abilities here." Behind us, I could hear Kat squawking, and Galok laughing. But their voices seemed so far away. As if the only ones left here were Taliok and me.

"Then I will help you up," Taliok rasped, a thick edge to his voice. I nodded wordlessly and felt him move even closer behind me. My nerves buzzed, and a hot pang of arousal sounded at his nearness. That pang turned into a deep pulse when Taliok put his hands on me. His hands fell to my hips, then moved upward to find the best grip to hoist me. But as he slid his hands upward, one of them caught on the hem of my tank top and my jacket, exposing a few inches of my bare, soft stomach. The rough pad of a finger and the sharp tip of a claw grazed my belly button. Taliok and I both froze at the realization that his finger was against my bare skin. My heart was a drum in my chest and in my head and in my pussy, an endless boom-boom-boom. Everything in my body screamed for him to *move*, to move that finger *lower*. Good fucking God, I couldn't deny it. I wanted him.

I barely breathed, and stopped breathing altogether, when that finger slowly circled the sensitive skin of my belly button again. A second ago, his touch on my skin had been accidental. But there was nothing accidental about the maddeningly soft, intentional slip of his fingertip now. I tensed, unable to keep myself from arching against that tiny, exquisite sensation. Taliok's other hand was like a vise on my body, and without thinking, I covered it with mine as I leaned back against him.

Taliok's breath shuddered out harshly against the hood of my jacket. The next thing I knew, he'd pulled his hand away and moved it up over my clothes again, gripping my waist firmly and lifting me easily up onto the saddle, like I weighed nothing. I gasped roughly as I landed on the contoured leather, like I'd been underwater and was just now coming up for air. Everything came back into focus – the sand, the sun, Galok and Kat on their irkdu nearby. I'd forgotten all of it existed. All of it, except Taliok.

And if that wasn't a truly, horrendously bad sign for how deep I was starting to fall, I didn't know what was.

12

TALIOK

I had never had my cock this hard for this long. It was turning to discomfort as we rode. I couldn't seem to calm my body or my mind. Having my fated mate, my love, this close, was addictive agony. Her stiff hood hid her face from me as she sat in front of me, and it dampened her scent, but it did nothing to relax me. Even though I could not see her face, my eyes kept coming back to her, before I wrenched them away to scan the sands for signs of predators. We were a small party, moving lightly and quietly, so it was unlikely we would attract scuttling zeelk up from beneath the sands. And herds of wild irkdu were rare. Krixel nested mainly in cliffs and high mountain ledges. But still, it would not do to get too distracted. As we trawled over the open sands, Galok and I kept weapons at the ready, looking around constantly. All around us was the open desert of the Sea Sands. There were a few landmarks, here. But I did not need them. I knew the way back to my homeland like it was etched into my very bones.

Gahn Buroudei's man, Galok, kept a lookout in between trying to force the other human woman, the small angry one with very little hair on her head, to converse with him. She rebuffed almost every effort, but I could not help but begrudgingly admire his tenacity. I wondered if I should be doing the same with Melanie – trying to talk to her again. But I did not know what to say. Or rather, all the things I wanted to say felt like they'd come out wrong. And besides that, we were within earshot of Galok and the woman Melanie called Kat. I did not want my words heard by anyone but my mate.

Not long into our journey, we passed the huge, shining shell that apparently had brought the new women from their world. In the sun, it looked like a silver corpse, but I had heard tell that the thing was not alive and had never been alive. How it could fly without being alive did not make sense to me. But so much about the new women did not make sense.

As we passed it, Melanie's head moved.

"What is it?" I asked.

She turned around in her saddle, looking at me from behind her strange black eye coverings.

"On the way back, can we stop at the ship?"

"The fallen thing that brought you here?"

"Yes," she confirmed. "There's equipment on board, and supplies we might need."

I glanced again at the hulking structure. The thing unnerved me, but if Melanie needed to go there, I would take her.

"Yes. We can go there."

Her lips pulled into a small smile.

"Thanks."

Then she turned around again, no idea at how much that one small change of expression had overwhelmed me.

We ate on our mounts and did not stop until the sun was beginning to bite at the horizon, darkness rising. We settled at an outcropping of boulders where some peet grass and babkit trees, the plants we often used for fires, grew. But as the meat I'd brought for us was smoked and dried, we did not need a fire.

Galok and I both leaped from our mounts to the sand. From the corner of my eye, I watched the angry Kat jump down herself, ignoring Galok's outstretched arms. She landed awkwardly and fell, cursing and rubbing her rump as she stood up. Meanwhile, Melanie had hooked one leg over the saddle so that she sat facing me. I reached up to grip her thighs.

"Slide forward. I will catch you."

She pushed her eye shells up over her forehead so that they rested on the top of her head and pulled back her hood. It was very good to see her lovely face again.

"OK. Don't drop me," she said.

She eyed the ground suspiciously, and I grunted, my hands tightening on her legs.

She thought that I would drop her, *could* drop her? Clearly, she did not yet trust me. And if she thought that me dropping her, or letting her fall, was even the slightest possibility, then she did not know me, either. *Patience Taliok.* She did not know me, *yet.*

She shimmied her hips forward, and I suppressed a groan at the sight of those curved hips rocking. Even through her clothing, the flesh of her legs felt perfect under my hands. It felt right. But I needed more...

Melanie bucked forward, sliding quickly off the mount. My hands moved up as her body came down, gripping her waist and bringing her easily to the ground. Even in the rapidly darkening air, I could see a slight stain of pinkness in her cheeks as she looked up at me.

"Thanks," she said, meeting my eyes. I grunted again, no longer capable of speaking. Having my hands on her like this was taking over my mind, and it left room for little else.

"Hi lovebirds, we gonna eat anytime soon?"

Melanie snatched herself out of my hands, turning and walking towards her friend who'd just spoken. I remained still, staring down at my empty claws for a moment before shaking myself back to my purpose. I quickly unpinned the satchels of dried meat and valok plants, passing the supplies out to the others.

"We will likely need to replenish before we reach my mountains," I said as I handed Galok a large selection of dried meat.

"I can go on a small hunt myself tomorrow while you continue on," Galok said seating himself next to a large black boulder. Kat then sat too, but not close to him. I waited for Melanie to sit, knowing that I would choose a place next to wherever she was.

Melanie sat next to her human friend, across from Galok, and I settled next to her.

"How long will this journey take?" Melanie asked, turning her dark eyes on me.

"At least one more day and night," I said, watching, fascinated, as Melanie's small jaw and lips moved, chewing some meat.

"Sounds good," she said, turning away and taking some valok. The pulse of her throat as she swallowed sent a sharp jolt to my cock. Holding back a growl, I adjusted my loincloth.

"Yes. We should get some rest soon," I said. I looked at Galok. "I only brought two tents."

When I felt Melanie stiffen beside me, I quickly explained.

"One for me, one for you and Kat to share."

She relaxed, but it was a spear of pain in me. Seeing how

relieved she was to not share a tent with me. But I reminded myself of my vow of patience. It was something I'd been known for all my life. And this was no different.

Except, it *was* different. I had never had to be patient for something I'd wanted this badly before. I'd never even wanted anything this badly before.

After eating, I set up my tent while Galok set up the one for Melanie and Kat. While working, he grinned at Kat.

"I will be sleeping right outside your tent if you should need anything," the young warrior said.

Even from the distance of a few paces away, I saw the roll of Kat's large blue eyes, that unnerving and uniquely human gesture.

As I drove the dakrival bone poles down into the sand for my tent, Melanie approached me, speaking softly.

"Do you need any help?"

Her voice was pure and shocking beauty. My whole body sprang into awakening for it.

"No."

My precious mate need have not concerned herself with work like this. I finished setting the poles, including the ones on the top, securing them all with leather bands and then draping hides over the structure.

"Looks cozy," Melanie remarked. She moved her head in that up and down motion I'd come to learn meant "yes." Was she agreeing with herself? I watched her, trying to decode every subtlety of her face and body. Trying to understand everything about her.

"Look, Kat, have I not built a good strong tent for your sleep?"

Galok's words drifted towards us, distracting my mate.

"Looks like our tent is ready to go," Melanie said. "I guess this is goodnight."

She licked her soft pink lips, and heat exploded under my

skin as I remembered those lips, that tongue, against mine last night. I stepped closer and leaned down, in case she wanted to do such a thing again. Her lips parted, and she made a small sound at my sudden nearness. I felt her breath against my face and bent even lower, drinking it in, every part of my body thrumming. My tail jerked on the sand behind me in anticipation.

But then more noise came from the others, and Melanie quickly pulled away. *I should have never allowed Kat and Galok to come,* I thought miserably as Melanie retreated to the other side of the little camp. I wanted Melanie all to myself.

But she did not want to be with me all by herself yet. So I would have to wait.

Kat entered their small tent. Melanie lifted the flap, then paused, turning back to me. I had not yet moved. I was still watching her.

She smiled softly, then raised a small hand, waving it in a gesture I did not understand. Then she disappeared behind the hides.

Galok settled himself on the sand, leaning back against a large boulder next to the tent he'd put up. I did not go into my own tent. I did not like the idea of being inside a tent, separated from my mate, while a warrior from another tribe was right outside where she slept. I trusted Gahn Buroudei's men more than Gahn Fallo's, but they were still not of my tribe. So far, Galok had proved himself to be a good sort of man, if somewhat foolhardy. But that did not mean he was allowed to sleep so close to Melanie if I wasn't there.

I approached the tent, sitting down across from him on the other side of it. He cracked an eye open at my arrival, then crossed his arms, settling further against the rock.

"I will sleep here," I said, my voice hard. If he registered the note of warning in it, Galok made no indication. He closed his eye again, getting ready to sleep.

"Of course, Gahn Taliok. I welcome the company."

My tail swished in response, and we fell into silence. Galok seemed to fall asleep quickly. It took me much longer to do so. But eventually, I too, drifted away, lulled by the fact that Melanie was sleeping safe, so close, at my side.

13

MELANIE

I woke up to the glow of the hot alien sun coming through the gaps in the tent's fabric. Stretching, I yawned, then wiggled my fingers and toes. I felt oddly refreshed. I'd slept better than I had in quite some time.

When I'd first heard Taliok outside the tent, telling Galok he would sleep there, my body had become a bundle of nerves at his proximity. But after a while, I'd relaxed into an almost eerie calm. For the first time in a long time, I felt... safe.

I just didn't know if I should trust it.

"Morning," Kat groaned, rubbing her eyes. We both sat up and started getting dressed.

"How'd you sleep?" I asked.

"Not bad." As she did up her pants, her gaze narrowed at me. "How about you? I didn't hear anything last night, so I assume Mr. Dark, Tall, and Scarred didn't try anything sketchy."

"No, of course not. He's a good guy," I said quickly.

He's a good guy? Where did that come from?

"Whatever you say," Kat said, slipping into her solar

protection jacket. I did the same, and then quickly slathered on some sunscreen from our rapidly depleting tubes.

When we stepped outside, we saw that Taliok and Galok were already ready. Taliok had already taken down his tent and was strapping it to his mount. I bit my lip, watching the cording of his muscles as he worked. When he finished, he turned, then noticed me. He rummaged through one of the satchels on the irkdu, then jogged over with valok gel and some more dried meat.

"Here, eat something before the journey," he said. His voice sounded softer than I'd ever heard it, and I felt myself flush.

"Thanks," I murmured, taking the food from him. As I did so, the tips of my fingers touched his palms, and I felt his whole body jolt at the touch. For a split second, I wished we were alone. More and more I was wanting to repeat the kiss from the other night.

And maybe even go further?

I was losing it. I was getting way too ahead of myself.

He's a good guy.

Those words had come so naturally when speaking to Kat. And they felt true and right. But dread sank low in my stomach as I remembered that I'd thought my ex, Greg, had been a good guy at first, too.

But Taliok was nothing like him. The more time I spent around him, the more sure about that fact I'd felt. But did that mean that I could truly trust Taliok, with everything? My body, maybe even my heart?

My questions were interrupted by Galok hurrying over to Kat, his hands similarly full of meat the way Taliok's had been.

"Look, Kat. I have already completed a fine hunt this morning and cooked you fresh meat."

"I don't eat breakfast," Kat snapped. I suppressed a smile, knowing full well that was a lie.

Galok didn't seem deterred.

"Then I will save it for when you are hungry."

Soon enough we were all packed and ready to go. Taliok lifted me onto the mount again, this time without any strangely sexy belly-button touching, and we got going.

The desert expanded all around us in an impressive and slightly terrifying spread of copper-gold. We hadn't been on the road long when a familiar sight came into focus on our right. As we kept going, I realized what it was.

"Are those Gahn Fallo's hills?" I asked turning my head slightly so Taliok would hear me better.

"Yes," he said, and the word sounded stiff and bitter. *He probably isn't going to like what I'm going to say next...*

"Can we stop there for a bit?"

Even though there was an inch of space or so between us, I felt Taliok tense at my back.

"Why?"

Maybe the request was a stupid one. But it was one I wanted to make all the same.

"They have lots of those soap cactus plants there. The long spindly ones."

Luckily we had those same plants at the Cliffs of Uruzai. The milky gel inside the long stalks proved to be an amazing soap, and their husks made for great toothbrushes. But neither Kat nor I had thought to bring them on our journey. I was scared to lift my arm for fear of what I'd smell there.

Taliok hadn't answered. *I knew he wouldn't like it.* But Kat piped up from Galok's irkdu.

"Yo, that sounds great. I want to stop, too."

"But it is Gahn Fallo's territory," Taliok ground out. I twisted to face him fully. His expression was stormy, his jaw set.

"We were with Gahn Fallo's tribe for a while before we moved to the cliffs. They won't do anything to us if we run into any guards. We'll be quick," I assured him.

Taliok's golden sight stars swirled, searching my face. From beside us, Galok piped up, "I will escort the new women, Gahn Taliok, if you do not wish to do so."

"No." Taliok's word was a forceful snarl as he looked over at Galok. Then he softened as he turned back to me.

"I am powerless against you. If you wish for this, then I will make it so."

Um. Wow.

I quickly spun to face forwards again so he wouldn't see the neon red glow that I was sure was radiating from my cheeks.

We moved quickly to the outer edges of Fallo's tribe's hills.

"We'll be quick," I promised again as Taliok helped me down to the sand. He grunted, but he didn't look happy, his eyes already scanning behind and around me.

"Come on," I said, and Kat and I jogged to the other side of the closest hill with our packs. Once on the other side, shaded by the hill, we stripped naked, then pulled some of the spindly cactus plants out of the ground and cracked them open. The smooth milky gel inside had a pleasantly sharp herbal smell to it, and it lathered into a smooth foam that we worked into our skin. As we cleaned ourselves, Kat spoke.

"So, you sure you're OK with everything so far? With Taliok and all that?"

I paused in my cleansing, mulling her question over. At first, the idea that I was Taliok's mate had bothered me. A lot. I wasn't ready for that, nor was I interested in it. And I still wasn't sure that I was ready to be anyone's mate. But as I thought over every interaction I'd had with Taliok so far, I had to admit that I was OK with what had happened between us. I was more than OK with it. With him. With everything. He had never pushed me, never asked anything of me. All he'd done was give me things – patience, time. Space, when needed. And it seemed lately like I was needing less and less of that.

"I am," I responded. It was an honest answer. I was finished cleaning my body, and I used the same soapy stuff to quickly scrub at the sweaty spots on my dirty clothes, laying them in the sun and dressing in the spare underwear and uniform I'd brought. I didn't have a spare bra, but I hoped that the one I'd just cleaned would dry quickly in the hot sun. Although, it was starting to look pretty ragged. *Wonder how much longer it will last...*

Kat was getting dressed now, too. Our eyes met.

"I could ask you the same thing," I said slowly. "About Galok."

She yanked the hood of her jacket up, then stuffed her hands into its pockets aggressively.

"Ugh. Don't even get me started on that guy. He's starting to get on my last nerve."

Concern mounted in me. I'd been half-joking, but I watched for Kat's response closely.

"Is he bothering you, really? We can switch. You can ride with Taliok if you want." I didn't really want to do that if I was being honest, but looking out for my friend was more important than me being with Taliok. But Kat was already shaking her head.

"No, it's fine. He hasn't said anything about this fated mate bullshit. He's annoying but harmless."

I nodded, thinking about how quickly she'd shut down my suggestion that we switch mounts.

Hmm.

"Speaking of annoying alien men, we should probably get back to them."

Kat was right. We'd been here a while, now. Taliok was probably chomping at the bit to get out of here.

Luckily my bra had mostly dried, and I snaked it on under my uniform before stuffing the clothes I'd cleaned into my pack.

"Ready?" Kat asked.

A frisson of excitement ran through me at the thought of seeing Taliok again, even though we'd basically just left him.

I nodded firmly in response to Kat's question.

"Yes."

1 4

TALIOK

"So, has she accepted you as her mate?"

My tail whipped, and I looked at Galok who had spoken beside me.

"You speak boldly to ask such things of a Gahn. Especially the Gahn of another tribe," I growled. He did not seem bothered by my words.

"Now that we have all moved to the Cliffs of Uruzai, it feels as though we are becoming one large tribe. I apologize if I was too forward. But I cannot help but be curious. She did not sleep in your tent…"

I grunted, turning my gaze back to the crest of the hill Melanie and Kat had gone over. I could hear their voices with my sharp ears. I knew they were alright. But being in Gahn Fallo's territory made my skin itch.

Galok decided, rather wisely for someone who seemed to have dung between his ears, not to press his question further. He raised his tail in apology, then bent to snap off a stalk of talka, the plant Melanie had called *soap*.

"I will clean myself, too, while we are here. I wish to be presentable for Kat."

He quickly stepped out of his loincloth and started lathering the talka gel over his skin. Suspicion began to mount in me. Why had he volunteered so eagerly for this journey?

"Has the Lavrika summoned you? Is Kat your mate?" Perhaps I should not have been so offended at his questions, earlier. Perhaps he was in the same position I was, with a strange new mate who did not want him. But he cut his hand through the air, his fingers shining with talka gel.

"No. I have not had the good fortune of being summoned yet. But this new woman, Kat... I like her. Even if she is not meant to be my mate, I wish to make a good impression during my time with her."

I grunted, trying to understand him as he cleaned himself diligently, scrubbing his scalp and running the talka through his long, unbraided hair. I had no interest in impressing any of the new women besides Melanie. And besides the fact that some of them may end up being mates to my men, I had very little interest in them at all. Only Melanie, with her serious dark eyes and steady, quiet intelligence made me want to get closer. So I did not understand Galok, with his preening for a woman who may not even be his mate. But then again, other men of the Sea Sands laid with women who were not their mates before getting summoned by the Lavrika. It was not so unusual. It just made no sense to me.

But perhaps I should take one note from Galok, I thought. I reached for my own stalk of talka, stripping out of my loincloth. I did not remove the straps and weapons from my torso, instead lathering between and beneath them.

I slipped the cleansing gel over my skin, scrubbing my scalp, my ears, down over my chest and under my arms, then lower, to my groin, before moving down my legs. I straightened quickly after that, scanning the area around us again, but there was no movement. No doubt Gahn Fallo had left a guard party in his territory the way I had. But his hills were vast, as were his people's plains and cliffs. So far, we had evaded notice. I would keep it that way.

But if we were noticed, if we were attacked, I'd kill every one of Fallo's men who dared to threaten my mate and me. And then I'd bring their heads back and toss them at Fallo's feet.

The thought was a good one. It made my tail twitch in satisfaction.

Galok used his empty talka stalk to clean his teeth. He spoke as he did so, the words muffled around the plant.

"I keep my hopes high for you that you will be successful in claiming your mate. It has been so long for so many of us."

His expression was relaxed, even easy. But there was pain in his words. A pain all the tribes of the Sea Sands shared. So many of us had resigned ourselves to life without a mate. I had always assumed that would be the life for me. But all that had changed now. I had Melanie, a shining joy that lit up the darkest corners of my life. Even if she did not accept me, never accepted me, I had more than many men did.

I grunted in thanks for Galok's words, deciding that I liked him.

I hoped that, soon, very soon, Melanie would decide she liked me, too.

15

MELANIE

"Jesus Christ!" Kat whirled around, facing back the way we'd just come, clamping her hands over her eyes.

Alarmed, I asked, "What, what is it?"

But then I saw what had caused her reaction.

Galok and Taliok were stark fucking naked. Obviously, they'd had the same idea we'd had, and were soaping themselves down. Heat flooded through my face, moving down my neck, then even lower as the two naked alien men heard Kat's commotion and turned towards us.

And, holy fucking shit. That… Was not an image I was prepared for this early in the day. The sight of Taliok turning, totally unabashed, to face me without any clothing at all. Well, besides his straps and weapons.

I gulped, my throat suddenly very, very dry. I tried to stop myself from letting my eyes go too low, but it was impossible.

Every inch of him was sculpted as if from dark marble. Perfect, hard muscle. And a massive, long, thick dark cock. I blinked several times, aware I was staring like an idiot, but I couldn't help it. He was a vision of masculine alien power and I couldn't fucking tear my eyes away. Especially when I noticed just how alien his cock looked. We were still some distance away, but it almost looked like there were... three?

Please, please don't tell me this guy has three fucking cocks.

I wasn't sure how I would deal with even the huge centre one, it was so big. But three?

Wait, are you planning to deal with it at all? Whether he has one weird cock or ten, it shouldn't matter to you.

But it did matter, apparently. Because even as I finally forced myself to whip around the way Kat had, my mind was overrun with thoughts of what I'd do to that cock. Or, cocks. Whatever it was that was going on down there, a primal urge had taken over. The urge to touch, explore. The urge to get him inside me.

I breathed heavily, trying to tamp down my insane urges. *Remember when you thought Taliok was the weirdo stalker? Now look at you, perv.*

Galok's voice suddenly next to us, greeting us, brought me back to reality somewhat. We turned to look at him, only to discover that he was still naked.

"Put on some fucking clothes, dude!" Kat yelped, shooing him away with her hands. He grinned widely, fangs gleaming, before striding back to grab his loincloth. A moment later, Taliok was at my side, speaking low.

"Are you ready to continue the journey?"

I nodded tightly, peeking down and to the side to make sure he was dressed. He was, but infuriatingly, it was both a relief and disappointment. My eyes slid over the bulge at his crotch, trying to piece together just exactly what I had seen a few moments ago. Not having a clear idea of what he was packing was frankly starting to eat at me.

He would show you up close if you asked him. You know he would.

I let out a small gasp and then clamped my mouth shut. *If*

these thoughts would kindly shut the fuck up for a bit, that would be great.

"What is wrong?" Taliok asked, leaning closer, his voice gruff with concern. My face was on fire. I couldn't look at him. But, God, I could smell him, the spicy scent of the cactus soap mixed with some sheen of raw masculine olfactory goodness. It was fucking with my head.

"Nothing. All good," I muttered, marching away from him and towards his irkdu. But walking away from him with such purpose was kind of pointless when he was just going to have to help me up onto the mount anyway. He did so without incident, but before I could start to relax in the saddle and talk myself down from the insane horniness that had apparently taken over my body, Taliok hoisted his huge frame up behind me. *Is it just me, or is he sitting a little closer than normal?* Every time he took a breath, I swore I could feel his chest brushing the fabric of my jacket. When he clicked his tongues to urge his irkdu into motion, I heard it literally right above me, as if his chin were above my head. Which, considering his height, it probably was.

We took off over the sands. Hours passed, and the land around us began to change. The copper and gold hues of the sand faded into a darker dusty red, and it became harder and flatter, packed down and cracked instead of soft and shifting like much of the desert we'd seen. Red rock formations grew out of the ground, getting larger around us. In the distance, even bigger formations were starting to come into view, but they were hazy in the distance.

"We have entered my people's territory. We will reach the mountains tomorrow," Taliok said against the side of my hood. I jumped, jerking my head to look at him beside me. But he had already pulled back, straightening and pointing his spear at a large outcropping of rock ahead of us.

"We will rest there for the night."

Galok made a noise of agreement, and we moved faster, speeding towards the large rock Taliok had indicated. The sky was starting to grow dark, and the asteroids were rising up on the horizon.

The rock we arrived at was like a tiny mountain in and of itself. At least thirty feet high, and coming to a pointed peak at the top. Taliok and Galok constructed the two tents under a rock overhang that provided some protection. We ate quickly and quietly on the ground, all of us tired from two days of hard travel. *At least we had the Zaphrinax version of a bath*, I thought to myself as I rubbed my stiff thighs. The saddle had helped things a lot, but riding for that long was definitely hard on the human girl bod.

"Are you in pain?"

Taliok's deep voice sent a jolt through me.

"A little. It's not bad. The saddle helped, thank you."

Taliok stared at my hands working over my sore quads. His sight stars expanded, swirling outward, growing hazy.

"May I help?"

I looked at him, not sure what he meant. But when his shifting golden eyes met mine, it clicked. *He wants to give me a fucking massage.*

My instinct was to immediately say no and scurry back to the tent. My gaze fell to his strong hands, and I found myself saying, "Yes, Please."

Taliok inhaled sharply, then rose to a crouch, moving towards me before sitting cross-legged again. With firm hands, he grabbed my ankles and yanked me forward so that my ass was right in front of his crossed shins, my thighs over his knees. My legs were spread to him, but I didn't have time to adjust the position. Because at that moment, those huge hands slid up to my thighs, beginning to knead my sore muscles through the fabric of my pants. I sucked in a hissing breath at the feeling, and he instantly stopped.

"Does it hurt?" There was a hard edge to his voice that hadn't been there before. And somehow his eyes looked darker.

"A bit. Go a little gentler?"

He grunted, then began again, much more gently this time, and I sighed, leaning back onto the palms of my hands on the ground behind me.

Somewhere nearby, I heard Galok trying to coax Kat into a leg massage, too, and she replied with what could only be described as a hiss. She loudly proclaimed that she was going to bed, and Galok settled himself in for the night against the rock on the other side of the tent, no longer in my line of sight.

I turned my attention back to Taliok, who was staring at his moving hands on my legs as seriously as if he were curing cancer.

"How is this? I do not wish to hurt you. You are so... *Soft*." His voice caught on that last word, like it was a hard stone in his throat. And that wasn't the only thing that was hard. I swallowed, seeing his loincloth straining.

"It's good," I whispered. And it was really fucking good. His strong fingers kneaded up and down my stiff muscles, producing the most pleasurable sort of pain. Heat moved outward from his fingertips, flooding my core. Flooding my pussy that was basically spread to him, just covered by clothing. I was aware of my breathing growing more shallow and quick. And Taliok's was getting heavier, more ragged.

His hands moved up, then down, then up, and up higher, until his thumbs were pressing at my inner thighs and his fingertips were massaging my outer hips.

"How about here? Is it good here?" he rasped, and this time I couldn't answer with words. I could only nod. Then I scooched forward and upwards until I was in his lap, settling into the diamond shape created by his crossed legs.

"There, now you can reach better," I said, throat tight. As if that was the only reason I'd moved into his lap. *You are in dangerous territory, girl. You are so fucking screwed...*

But then Taliok's hands slipped back further and started kneading my ass with barely controlled abandon, and any thoughts of danger or stopping this went out the goddamn window. Taliok groaned against the top of my head, and I felt his cock, or cocks, or whatever, jump against the front of my pants.

It would be so easy to reach down there...

I shifted forward slightly until his hardness was pressed perfectly against my clit. Desire slammed through me, and I couldn't ignore it. Not anymore. It's like I was stranded in the middle of the ocean, and the tide had just turned and was pulling me under. There was no fighting it.

"Melanie..." My name was a guttural growl against my hair, and it sent a sharp bolt of heat between my legs. I reached downward, ready to shift Taliok's tight loincloth to the side...

When a commotion behind me made me jump so hard that I leapt right out of Taliok's lap. A strong hand caught my arm and kept me from falling flat on my ass as I scrabbled off of his legs. Shimmying out of his hold, I turned to see Kat emerging from the tent.

"I forgot I had to pee," she announced. She leaned around the tent to the other side where Galok was laying. "Don't follow me."

She stomped around the rock formation until we couldn't see her. I was aware of Taliok's glinting eyes on me, but I couldn't look at him. I was scared of what I'd see there. Intense desire. Maybe even love. *I shouldn't have let it get this far.*

"I should probably go to bed," I said.

"You need rest," he admitted slowly. I nodded, then stood,

tossing out a quick goodnight as I jogged over to the tent. Just as I was heading inside it, I heard his deep, steady voice from behind me.

"Goodnight, Melanie from beyond the stars."

I didn't have time to bask in the beauty of the nickname he'd created for me. Because a moment later, Kat came bursting back in and flopped down onto her hides.

"Damn, I'm beat. Time to hit the hay."

If she had seen me getting all hot and bothered with Taliok in the darkness, she didn't say anything. And something told me that if she had seen it, she would definitely say something. But no, she just rolled over and more quickly than should have been possible, started to snore. Outside the tent, I could hear Taliok shifting, getting into position to sleep next to my side of the tent. Warmth expanded in my chest at the thought of him out there, staying by me. And that warmth was different than the heat of a few moments ago. It was safety, it was comfort. It was the beginning of trust.

It was true. I was starting to trust him. And that thought suddenly didn't scare me as much as it once did.

I undressed and laid down, pressing close to the fabric of the tent, as if I could feel Taliok through the wall. I closed my eyes, but I couldn't fall asleep. I was too aware of his presence outside. And my body was still thrumming with our earlier interaction.

This is stupid. If you want to spend more time with him, then go do it.

There was that voice again. Telling me all the things I didn't need to hear.

Or maybe I *did* need to hear them. Holding my breath and being as quiet as possible, I rose and dressed, then stole out of the tent.

Taliok was lying on his side, his head supported on his arm, facing the tent. But he was up in an instant when he noticed me, drawing himself to his full height, like a fucking monster from a fairy tale. But one of the fairy tales where the princess falls in love with the monster.

Whoa. Falls in love with?

"Melanie," he said quietly. I couldn't get enough of my name in his mouth. It was desire and intensity and a promise of things to come. A promise of forever. Leaning into that voice, leaning into him and everything he had to offer, I whispered,

"Can we go to your tent?"

I didn't even need to bother asking. Because when Taliok heard my question, his answer was instantaneous.

"Yes."

16

TALIOK

Melanie wanted to come to my tent.

As I led her over to where I had set up my tent and lifted the flap for her, I tried not to dwell on questions of what it meant. I focused only on her. Her, right now, in this moment.

I moved behind her into the tent. It was much, much smaller than the kind of tent our people would live in. This was a tiny structure meant for travelling. And it was pitch black. The hide cut off any glow of star or moonlight. Melanie was a shapeless shadow, and that bothered me. I wanted to see her. Make sure this was real. She was real.

"I brought a valok candle," I said, turning from her and rummaging in the supplies I had stored in the corner of the tent.

"Great," she said. Her voice sounded strangely breathy. Once again, I fought down questions of what it meant. But this time it was much harder. My heart was a deep pounding. Every part of my skin buzzed.

I lit the valok candle with the fire rocks I had brought,

then placed the small flame back down in the corner. The inside of the tent jumped to flickering life.

Melanie was real. She was here.

But why?

I could not help the flush of blood to my cock at the hope that this meant she finally accepted me as her mate. My eyes traced her bare shoulders, the thin straps of her strange sleeveless tunic, down to her chest. The pull of her heavy breasts there had me forcing down an urgent growl. She was all softness. All beauty.

But now that she was here, she didn't seem to know what to do. She looked around, crossing her arms. This pressed her round breasts upward, and I had to stop myself from staring the way I knew she hated.

We remained in silence for a long moment, Melanie looking everywhere but me and me looking nowhere but her. Finally, I could not take it anymore.

"Why did you want to come here?"

She jumped at my words, her dark eyes flashing to mine. She rubbed her hands over her elbows.

"I just... I wasn't ready to say goodnight yet."

I grunted and moved closer, stepping right up to her chest and leaning down.

"Are your legs still sore?"

In the candlelight, I could see redness blooming on her cheeks. Fascinated, I reached up and stroked the pad of my finger across one cheek, then the other. I marvelled at the plush silkiness. To my utter joy, she leaned into the touch.

"Yeah, actually. If you don't mind..."

Mind? It would be my greatest honour and pleasure to massage any part of my mate. The fact she did not know this was a tragedy.

So I told her.

"It would be my greatest honour and pleasure to massage any part of you."

Curse me. My voice was unrecognizable, a feral beast's growl. But Melanie did not seem to be bothered. She sat on the sand. I did too, crossing my legs and pulling her legs over my knees once again.

I ran my hands over her knees to her supple thighs. My hands covered more than half the area between her knees and hips. These women were truly tiny. I had a dark moment of doubt that, should Melanie accept me as mate, my cock would not fit inside her. But Gahns Buroudei and Fallo had human mates, and I had heard no tell of injury from mating them.

Do not get ahead of yourself.

I was here to service my Gahnala. She had not yet accepted me as her mate. *Do not think of yourself so much. Think only of her.*

I focused, pressing my fingers in a kneading motion, being careful not to go too hard. My natural strength coupled with her softness was difficult to manage. She was so delicate. I had to be careful.

"Oh, that feels good."

My cock jumped. I cast my sight stars up to Melanie's face. It was still flushed red, and her head was tilted, her eyes grown hazy. My gaze fell to her wet pink mouth, but I had to tear it away. Looking at that perfect mouth and not tasting it was a pain, deep in my body. So I looked back down at my hands.

A moment later, Melanie began wiggling, shifting forward on the sands. She slid up until she was in my lap the way she had been before. And I wanted to fall to my knees in gratitude at the perfection of it.

But it was also perfect agony. Her small hands were on my shoulders, her breasts brushing my chest. Her cunt, *curse me*, was pressed against the aching underside of my shaft, which arched up in its hardness.

"This is better," she breathed.

"Yes." She was right. This was better. This was better than anything I'd ever known. If just being close to her brought me such joy, what would being inside her feel like?

I kept working on her legs, my hands moving back to her hips, then the curve of her rump. Melanie gave a small gasp at that, and my hands tightened involuntarily, drawing her closer, pressing her harder against my cock. My head fell forward, my nose burying in her hair. I tried to control my breathing, control the tightness of my hands. But it was difficult. So difficult.

Melanie's hands were moving now, tracing tiny lines of jumping fire over my skin. A low groan built in my throat at the brutal pleasure of it. The tantalization. Surely, she did not know what she was doing to me. She did not seem cruel. Everything I had seen of her showed her to be thoughtful, especially for the needs of others. But her touch was bringing me to the point of madness. Of death. It was too much and not enough all at once.

But I would take whatever I could get. My breathing grew ragged as her fingers moved. They were mostly touching my right side – my neck, my shoulder. *She's tracing my scars.*

"I feel like I should tell you that Exoka – the Fol-Gahnala – told me how you got these."

I flinched, my hands stopping moving for a moment.

"I hope that's alright," she added quickly.

Melanie pulled back to look into my face. The look of concern there was a genuine one. *No, my mate is not cruel. She is soft-hearted.*

"It is not a story I like to think of," I said. "But I do not mind that she told you. All in my tribe know of it." I gently brushed a strand of dark hair away from her pale forehead. "And there is nothing that I would hide from you."

She took a sharp breath and moved her head up and down. Her eyes shifted to my bent ear, and her fingers followed, traipsing lightly over my mangled skin.

"Do they bother you?" I had to ask. Of course, there was nothing I could do about them now. But the ember of not knowing how she felt about them, about me, was beginning to burn a hole in my guts.

"No!" She said it forcefully, flattening her hand against my scarred right cheek. Then, more softly, "No. Not at all. I mean, I would rather you didn't have them because I know they mean you've suffered. But they don't bother me."

My hands moved up to her waist, pulling her yet closer. I groaned and lowered my forehead against hers.

"Good."

I felt the breath of her next question against my mouth.

"How old were you when your father died?"

I did not know how the human women measured such a thing. I tried to think of a child she would know of that would be similar.

"There is a healer of Gahn Fallo's tribe. She has a young son. He is about the right age," I said.

Melanie gasped and yanked back, her eyes wide, her slim dark brows drawing downward.

"Bokeelie's son?!"

That sounded right.

"I believe so," I replied.

She shook her head, her small mouth falling open.

"It's hard to tell ages because you guys are so much bigger than humans, but I would place him at like eight or nine years old by human standards, at most."

I grunted. Those numbers meant nothing to me. But clearly, they meant something to Melanie. Her eyes grew glossy. One bead of shimmering liquid trailed down her cheek. I reached up and caught it, staring at the shine of the wetness on my thumb.

Last time this had happened she said it was because she had heard something very sad.

"I have upset you," I grumbled. The moisture on my thumb sank into my skin, and I felt a small thrill. Part of her was in me now. Always.

"You didn't upset me," she said. "But that's a terrible thing to have had happen as a child. It must have been very hard."

It had been hard. Killing the krixel as a small child had been hard. Dragging my father's heavy body for days, back to our people was hard. It had taxed my young body and left me scarred. But I had a feeling that was not what she meant.

"It is done," I said simply.

She nodded.

"I understand. I have things like that in my past, too. Things that you can't change but just... Have to move on from."

A shadow of pain crossed her fair features. I bent my face even closer, on alert. My voice almost sounded angry when I spoke next. Perhaps I was angry. The thought of Melanie suffering made me want to kill something.

I growled, almost right against her mouth, my hands hot and hard at her back.

"What things?"

1 7

MELANIE

"What things?'

The question hung in the air between us. It was kind of like Taliok's cock in that it was pressing and could not be ignored. *Am I really going to do this? Spill my sob story to an alien I barely know? A story I haven't told anyone else?*

But it didn't feel like I didn't know Taliok. Not anymore. Day by day, piece by piece, I was building an image of him. Scar by scar, he was coming into focus.

And I had to admit, I really fucking liked what I saw.

I took a steadying breath. *Fuck it.*

"You lost your parents because they died. I lost mine because they abandoned me."

Taliok's brows contracted at my words, but he said nothing, waiting for me to continue. Goddamnit. This had never been my strong suit. Talking. Sharing. I was always the watcher, the observer, the listener. But Taliok was pulling it out of me.

"A lot of this will be hard to understand," I began. "There are cultural differences that won't make sense to you, but I'll do my best to explain and keep it short." Taliok grunted and I continued. "My parents were very… Strict. Where I come from, there are many different religions and many different gods. My parents followed a very strict form of a religion called Christianity. They were very controlling throughout all of my childhood. And by adolescence, I'd had enough. I started rebelling. I refused to go to church." That had been my parents' biggest shame, at that point. "But it got worse. I told them I wanted to study geology. I'd always loved rocks and the earth and the history packed into all that. But they refused. It challenged their worldview too much. They believed in the Biblical history of the world, and thousands of years of geology didn't fit into that."

Taliok's sight stars had pulled tight, and his brow had furrowed even lower. He was trying so hard to figure out what the hell I was saying. Even I barely knew. I'd never put all these words together. They were probably coming out all wrong. But Taliok wasn't judging me or demanding things of me, just listening. So I kept going.

"In my last year of high school, around the time they were up in arms over my school choice, I started dating my cousin's neighbour."

Taliok's eyes narrowed.

Yikes. I'm not going to get away without explaining that one a little better. He's way too smart. He knows it's a guy.

"Dating is like… doing… mating things with someone before you decide they're your mate."

Taliok's breath hitched, and his tail jerked. I flinched, waiting for anger, but none came. With what looked like a great show of will, he forced his expression into something fairly neutral.

"Please continue," he growled. "I wish to know it all. Everything about you. Everything there is."

Nodding, I plunged onward.

"My parents found out about this… mate." That was a sugar-coated way of putting it. They'd found a packet of condoms in my bedroom after raiding it the way they always fucking did and they'd gone ballistic. "They kicked me out. They disowned me."

Taliok's eyes flashed, and now there was true anger there.

He looked like he wanted to say something, but he gnashed his teeth.

"Continue." His voice was even lower, now.

"I had nowhere else to go," I said. "And I was feeling spiteful. So I moved in with my boyfriend… or, mate. My birthday is early, in January, and I was eighteen. I was an adult and could start my own life. And my parents completely cut off contact." I refrained from repeating the horrible things they'd told me – that I was a sinner, that I'd been claimed by demons, that unless I welcomed Christ back into my life I'd never be welcomed in theirs. There wasn't much point telling Taliok all this. He had no context for any of those things – no idea about Christ or church or any of it. So I kept going, sticking to the core of the story. *Just give him the basics and get it over with.*

"Well, this… mate. He wasn't a good man. He wasn't a good mate." Once again, that was sugar-coating it. The lies, the gaslighting, the infidelity and bouts of anger. It went on for two years, but when he threw a plate at my head during a fight, I knew I had to leave. I still remember how fast I'd packed when he'd gone to sleep for the night, my hands shaking in the panicked dark. "So I left him," I said finally.

Taliok's hands had turned to iron on my back.

"I need to hear exactly how he was not a good mate," he snarled, his voice shuddering as if he was fighting to keep it even. I gave a short, humourless laugh.

"If you're trying to take notes so you don't make any of the same mistakes, you don't need to worry." It was true. At first, I'd been afraid that Taliok would turn out like Greg. In the beginning, Greg had been all charm and love, too. But where Greg had laid it on thick to manipulate me, Taliok was all sincerity. He was dark and quiet, like me, but everything he'd done had shown me that he was legit.

"That is not why I asked," he said. "I need to know if he has hurt you. If he has, I will find a way back to your world and tear his head from his shoulders, tossing it at your feet where it belongs.'

All sincerity. Yup. One look at the twisted look on his face told me he was telling the absolute truth. I shook my head, placing my hand on his chest.

"He wasn't a good mate. He wasn't kind. But he never physically hurt me. It never got to that. But I thought it might, one day, so I left."

Taliok's lips curled back from his fangs.

"I should kill him for not being good to you, then bring him back to life just so I can kill him again for his sheer stupidity. Anyone who does not treasure you for what you are does not deserve to breathe."

Jesus. Was it bad that his words were extremely fucking appealing?

Let's get off this topic.

I stopped, wondering if I should tell him the next part. But I couldn't think of any real reason not to. He might as well know the whole story.

"When I left Greg, I was halfway through my undergrad degree. Um... My training. And I needed money." Oh, God. How was I going to explain Earth capitalism? *Too much for tonight.* I forged forward, hoping he wouldn't need too many details about the economics of life on Earth. "My parents had never let me have a job, and I'd gone right from their house to living with Greg and surviving on scholarships. But those scholarships only covered tuition, nothing else. I didn't have any skills. So... I became a cam girl."

I paused with bated breath, waiting for shock, judgment, disgust. But there was none. *Is that because Taliok is such a truly kind and understanding guy? Or is it because he doesn't know what a cam girl is?*

When I didn't say anything else, Taliok asked, "What is a cam girl?"

There was no way I'd be able to explain the internet and porn and computers to Taliok. *Sparknotes version, Mel.*

"It's... It's someone who undresses in front of others for their pleasure."

Taliok cocked his head, mouth tightening.

An idea overtook me, and once it entered my brain, I couldn't get it out.

"Here, it's easier if I show you."

I wriggled out of Taliok's arms and lap, scooting away from him. He tracked my every move with glinting eyes. I moved up onto my knees, then ran my hands through my hair, twisting my hips suggestively as I did so. Taliok's eyes fell down my body, his jaw hardening.

"You just sit there, and I'll show you what I'm talking about," I whispered.

Was this fucking real? Was I about to give Taliok the show of his goddamn life right now in this tent? I'd never been ashamed of my work as a cam girl. My rebellion from my parents' tight hold had refused to let me feel ashamed. It had been a part of reclaiming my independence and my sexuality. It had gotten me through some shitty fucking times, and kept my bank account fat while I rebuilt my life. But I had never anticipated that I'd be showing this side of myself to someone I knew in person.

But I really fucking wanted to. I wanted to undress for

Taliok. I wanted to see his gaze cloud over with even more desire. And I really wanted to see what would happen next.

I shook my hair back over my shoulders, still swaying on my knees. Then I ran my hands up my front, cupping my heavy breasts and squeezing, then jiggling them. The catch in Taliok's throat as he swallowed was visible even from here, and as his eyes sank to where my hands grasped my flesh, heat exploded inside me.

Without thinking, I reverted into some of my usual cam girl lines.

"Oh, yeah, do you like that?"

Taliok's nostrils flared.

"Yes."

I blinked, kind of forgetting that he could hear me and that he'd actually answer. But his honesty, the unabashed eagerness in his answer, made my pussy clench. I bit my lip, feeling my nipples harden through my bra, under my palms.

Fuck it. I'm doing this.

"Do you want to see some more?"

Once again, the answer was instant, though his voice cracked slightly on the word this time.

"Yes."

I slipped my tank top's straps over my shoulders and then shimmied the garment down to my hips. I started massaging my breasts again, only wearing a bra. Taliok's gaze was fucking glued to my hands. And it felt really good. I felt beautiful and powerful and seen. And I felt like I was totally in control. If it wanted to stop this, I could. And I knew Taliok would let me.

But I don't want to stop this.

Wordlessly this time, I undid my bra, pulling it off then tossing it somewhere behind me. Taliok let out a choked sound, and his cock visibly leapt beneath his loincloth. Fuck, that hardness was insane. It looked fucking huge. Not to mention that I recalled seeing more than one…

Taliok was still sitting cross-legged, and his claws dug ferociously into the sand. A thrill went through me when I realized he was clutching at the ground so hard to keep from touching me.

He's such a good boy.

Good boy? Jesus.

But that was just the phrase that came to mind. Not that he was anything like a boy. Now, he was seven feet of pure alien man.

I circled my puckered nipples with slow fingers, feeling tingles and sparks shoot all the way down into my pelvis. When I'd done shows before, I'd had toys and lube and all kinds of things to bring the arousal to its peak. But I'd never felt as turned on as I did now. In fact, I couldn't remember a time I'd ever felt this aroused, with any partner, ever.

"Fuck, I'm so horny."

Taliok was still staring at my breasts, watching the slip of my fingers over my skin. But he swallowed, hard, then asked, "What is *horny*?"

I choked back a grin. He really was a good boy. He was trying to show me that he was listening to what I was saying. But it was clear that formulating words was kind of difficult for him right now. His jaw worked, his chest heaved. As I watched his claws clench further down into the ground, I realized that there was no fucking way he was getting out of this without touching me.

Just not yet.

"It means aroused," I whispered, undoing the button at the top of my pants.

"Ah," Taliok said, but the word came out strangled. His pectoral and ab muscles bulged as he tensed, watching me slip my pants down over my hips. I moved one hand back up to my breast, then let the other fall between my legs, brushing my clit. I cried out, unable to stop myself. Taliok's tail thrashed behind him, and his lip quivered in a snarl over his fangs. But he still hadn't moved to touch me. Hadn't crossed any lines.

At this rate, I'm going to be the one begging him to fuck. I moved my hand faster against my clit, feeling my panties growing wet. Taliok's cock twitched again, pulling his loincloth.

"I'm getting so wet," I murmured. Taliok tore his eyes from my moving hands to look at my face in confusion.

"Your skin is dry."

I licked my lips and shook my head.

"No, not my skin. I'm wet *here.*" I lowered my other hand so that both were between my legs, and I rocked forward, grinding against them, moaning softly. Then I stopped and caught his gaze again. "Want to see?"

"Yes. Yes," Taliok said it twice, as if to make sure I had heard. To make sure the word hadn't gotten lost somewhere between his brain and his mouth. It was completely fucking charming.

Is he a virgin?

A new thrill ran through me. The thought that I might be this mighty warrior's first. His first love, his first pussy, his first everything. But how on Earth, or Zaphrinax, could a gorgeous warrior like him be a virgin? I knew there weren't a lot of women around here, but still. It didn't seem possible

"Taliok, tell me. Have you ever been with a woman like this before?"

Taliok's tail twitched. His golden eyes were pulsing.

"No. I have never lain with a woman."

Goddamnit. That was too cute. I couldn't stand it. It made me want to do so much for him, show him so much, give him so much.

145

He took a shaking breath, speaking quickly.

"But if you are concerned by my lack of experience, please know that I have always been a diligent student. I have trained harder than any man. Anyone in my tribe will tell you this. I will be the most faithful student this world has ever seen. If you will teach me."

My mouth dropped open. This guy, this insanely huge, muscled, alien warrior was basically telling me he'd be a scholar of my fucking body. A scholar in the field of giving Melanie orgasms. His face was so serious it looked like he was applying for his PhD. That was more than any man on Earth had ever offered me. I almost couldn't believe he'd said it. But this was Taliok. And it was such a perfectly Taliok thing to say. So I did believe it. Every word.

"This is your first lesson," I breathed, rolling my panties down. I shifted onto my ass, peeling my remaining clothing off my ankles and putting it aside. *Here we go.* There was no backing out now. I was stark naked in front of Taliok. But I didn't want to back out. I wanted to see this through. See just how studious he was really going to be.

Settling into a sitting position with my legs drawn demurely in front of me, I looked at Taliok. He was sitting up even higher now, his spine ramrod straight.

I let my knees fall open to my sides.

Taliok's nostrils flared, but he was silent as he stared between my spread legs. I slipped my fingers back down through my wetness, loving the way his eyes tracked my fingers hungrily. As if he wished it were his tongues.

"This is a human woman's pussy," I said, dragging the tips of my fingers towards my entrance back up. "And this," I said, my breath catching as I brushed the top of my folds, "is a clit. It feels really good to touch it." To emphasize my point, I circled that small bit of swollen flesh, arching my back against the sensation. Oh my God, I was already ready to come soon. Taliok's gaze was laser-focused between my legs.

I shifted closer on the sand until I was up against Taliok's shins. His sight stars were blown wide open as he looked from between my legs to my face.

"You should come closer," he growled. "So I can study better."

I nodded quickly. I wouldn't want my poor student straining his eyes. Once again, I moved into his lap. Then I leaned back, one hand against the sand in front of his ankles. I was basically lying in the web created by his crossed legs, and I hooked my hips upward, spreading my legs wide so that he could see it all.

His chin buried itself in his chest as he stared downwards. In this position, his cock was pressed firmly upward between my ass cheeks. With a small gasp, I moved further forward, pressing against it, eliciting an animalistic groan from Taliok that I felt in my deepest core.

"You can try," I said suddenly, the words almost not making it out of my mouth they were so high and almost squeaky. "You'll never be a good student if you don't practise."

Was I seriously inviting an alien to start playing with my pussy?

Yes. Yes I was

But this wasn't just any alien. This was my Taliok.

My Taliok.

It kind of felt good to say it.

Taliok didn't need any more encouragement than that. He raised a huge hand, brushing his claws through my curls. I moved my own fingers out of the way, waiting to see what he'd do, barely breathing.

Taliok curved his torso forward, bending closer and inhaling deeply. I felt a deep flush of embarrassment at that, but my scent only seemed to turn Taliok on more. He groaned again. His other hand that had been clutching at the sand jumped up to grip my hip.

He moved his fingers down from my pubic area to the top of my pussy. The rough, warm pad of his thumb brushed my clit, and it was like an electric fucking shock. I jolted, crying out, and Taliok withdrew his hand immediately.

"Don't stop," I panted. Taliok replaced his hand without speaking. His jaw was clenching so hard I could see the muscles bulging at the sides of his face and down his neck. He brushed my clit again, then pressed gently, and then more firmly, moving his thumb from side to side, then in circles, as if testing which way was best. Apparently, they were all the fucking best, because my head rolled back against his ankles. My hair dragged through the sand and my hips started grinding. I gripped Taliok's forearms, marvelling at the smooth skin and metal-strong muscles beneath it. He was so freaking strong. And in this moment, I could tell he was channelling every facet of that strength into iron-clad control. He was keeping himself back, only doing what I asked him to do.

A rush of affection surged through me. And that rush intensified when he spoke.

"Your loveliness is beyond compare. Beyond imagining. I am... haunted by it."

I raised my head to look at him, and good God he did look haunted. He looked totally... Lovesick. His eyes bored into mine with an intensity that made everything in me clench.

Fuck. I want to see him.

I sat up in his lap, moving my hands to his shoulders, then down to his chest. I brushed my hands over his nipples and felt his cock strain even further.

I glanced down at his loincloth. *Good thing that dakrival*

hide is so strong. Taliok's cock, or cocks, or whatever the hell he was packing, looked like it was hard enough to cut through stone.

I inhaled sharply, licking my lips, knowing I couldn't take back the next words and not caring.

"You should take that off."

18

TALIOK

I had reached the hardest edge of pleasure. And insanity. Melanie pressed against me in my lap, naked and waiting and wet. *So* wet, dripping onto my fingers as I stroked her, exploring her. I had thought other parts of her were soft, but this was even more so. Slick and silky and waiting for my cock.

And Melanie had just told me to remove my loincloth.

I did so, undoing the garment and tearing it away with one shaking hand, not willing to remove the other from Melanie's heat. She made a sound and stared.

"What is it?" I asked. She shook her head in that odd human way. Sometimes that movement indicated displeasure, and I was dismayed.

"Does my cock displease you?"

Her slim brows shot up and she looked into my face.

"No! That's not it. It's just... Different from human men. There are three..."

I looked down, too, as her gaze returned to my cock. I had never heard of a man with three cocks. Did such a thing exist in her world? No, I had one cock, and like all men of the

Sea Sands, the cock spears: two shorter, more pliable bits of flesh on either side of it. The cock spears only came about halfway up the length of my cock.

"Only this is my cock," I said, using my free hand to stroke up the hardness. Her eyes flared as I did so, and my pelvis jerked.

"Oh," she said softly. "Looks like I need to be a student, too.

The thought was laughable. My beautiful, intelligent Melanie, learning anything from me? Impossible.

A new glint took hold in her eyes, and she moved one of her small hands from my shoulder. Her fingers brushed my tip, so softly I thought I'd die if she didn't go harder. If I didn't get inside her soon.

I moved my hand out of her way, settling it against the smooth skin of her back while my other hand continued to slick through her wetness. I longed to plunge a finger, or even two or three, inside her. But my claws would harm her, perhaps irreparably. They would do too much damage. So I contented myself with the brush of my fingers on the outside of her body, aching to know what she felt like inside.

Melanie gripped my shaft, beginning to stroke up and down in a rhythm that made me buck against her hand. She gave a small moan, then brought her other hand down, fondling my cock spears at the same time, bringing explosive heat throughout my groin. The scent of her arousal over-whelmed me, thickening the air, making me want her more than I would have thought was possible. My hips bucked up again, of their own accord. I shifted my grip against Melanie's wet cunt, and brushed her clit with my knuckle.

She moaned sharply, then huffed, "OK, I can't take this anymore. Lie back."

I did as instructed, and hoped mightily that by "I can't take this anymore" she didn't mean she wanted to stop. She hooked her legs on either side of my hips, placing her hands on my abdomen. Her brows contracted slightly as her hand caught on one of my weapons' straps.

"You don't need to wear these with me, you know."

She meant my weapons. I could feel the flats of the blades of my back pressing against my skin. My hands ran up the silk of her thighs to her hips.

"I do need to. Especially with you. To protect you." It was difficult to speak. Difficult to think with Melanie hovering over me the way she was. She didn't look convinced by my words, however, so I added more. "Once we are in my mountains, deep in my territory, I can remove them in my tent.'"

"OK," she said. She wiggled her hips just below my cock, her wetness coating my balls.

"I don't think I'm ready to go all the way. Um. To mate tonight. But I just need to..."

She shifted her weight forward, rolling her hips and dragging her pussy against the underside of my cock, forcing the hard flesh down towards my abdomen with her weight. I could not stop the hard moan that escaped my throat. That pressure, that wetness... It was exquisite. It was almost painful in its perfect pleasure.

"God, you're so hard," she whispered. She adjusted slightly, putting more of her weight onto her hands on my abdomen, then began rocking the slickness of her cunt up and down the underside of my cock. I gripped her hips, her ass, as she rode me, grinding harder and faster. The crimson of her cheeks was beautiful, her scent unbearable. I was coming undone. Every time her cunt slipped up towards my tip, I longed to plunge myself inside her. But she had said she was not ready. So I did not.

I smoothed my hands along her waist. I wanted to grasp her round breasts. I wanted to heft their softness, feel the taut nipples. But my large hands would block my view. And that view was a spectacular one – that rolling flesh bouncing as she moved.

Eventually, the need to touch her won out over needing to see her. My hands moved up, tightening against her incredibly soft mounds. A brutal growl ripped from my throat, and her nipples hardened further under my palms. I should not have worried about the view. The view of my hands on her flesh was even more erotic. I could not believe this was happening, that she was with me now, that those were indeed my hands on her perfect body. I had a mate. Me, scarred Taliok of the mountains, had a mate. And slowly, surely, she was coming to accept me, opening to me like a rindla flower at dawn.

Melanie leaned into my touch, pressing herself into my hands and groaning, rocking her hips faster. My own pelvis was arching up, over and over again, to meet her movements. Pleasure built, a hot pull, deep in my groin, spreading outwards and upwards. Need took over. My hands snapped back down to her hips, gripping her hard and holding her in place as my pelvis drove against her with a ferocious speed I did not know I was capable of.

Melanie released herself to the sensations, to my cock against her folds, stopping her own motion and remaining frozen above me. A long, low mewl escaped her lips. Her fingers clenched into fists on my abdomen

"Fuck, Taliok, I'm coming!" She threw her head back, no longer holding still. Her hips writhed in my grip, her eyes rolling back, her wet mouth open. Watching her give in to the pleasure was my undoing, and with a bit-back roar I exploded, rope after rope of glistening seed coating Melanie's breasts and soft stomach. Some of it even shot as high as her throat. She gleamed with it, and I groaned at the sight. The sight of my seed glittering on Melanie's skin. Marking her.

I wanted to mark her even more. I wanted to claim her, *inside*.

But for now, I was grateful.

There would be time for more.

And I was a patient Gahn.

19

MELANIE

I sank down against Taliok's pelvis, every muscle turning into overcooked noodles. My chest rose and fell raggedly as pleasure pulsed through me, echoes of one of the best orgasms I'd ever had. Taliok's grip softened, just slightly, against my hips.

I couldn't move. And that wasn't an exaggeration about not wanting to move. I literally could not fucking move. My muscles had gone to utter shit after that.

"Taliok?" I croaked, my thighs quivering. The guy was so big my knees barely reached the ground on either side of him. "Can you help me get off?"

Ha! He'd certainly done that already.

In an instant, Taliok sat up, gingerly lifting me away and then down to the sands beside him. With a groan, I collapsed onto my back, letting my limbs sag heavily into the ground, eyes closing. A moment later, the drag of leather against my skin made them shoot open again.

Taliok was kneeling next to me with a bit of leather left-over from the tent construction. He smoothed it over my skin, all the way up from my pubic bone to my throat.

What the hell is he doing? Is this some Sea Sands, post-orgasm ritual?

He caught my questioning gaze.

"It looks beautiful on your skin. But I imagine it is not comfortable."

Oh my God. He was wiping his fucking cum off of my skin. He truly was already a thousand times better than any human man I'd ever been with. He made me feel like a queen.

Because to him, you are a queen.

I flushed at that thought. I was his Gahnala, right? The queen of his tribe? At least, he wanted me to be.

But what did I want?

One thing was for sure, I didn't want this feeling to end. This feeling of being treasured, cherished, desired. Loved.

He kept going with the leather fabric, taking extra care around my breasts and against my nipples. As my sensitive skin pricked, I realized he was probably taking a little too much care, there.

"I think I'm all clean, now," I said, feeling a slight smile play about my lips. Taliok tossed the rag in the corner of the tent before lying down next to me. He laid the same way he had been when I found him outside earlier tonight. On his side, his head resting on his arm, facing me. I turned on my side, too, to face him. Then I nuzzled closer, snuggling into the broad wall of his chest. It felt so good. So safe and warm and cozy.

Before I knew it, I was drifting. The last thing I was aware of was the heavy drape of Taliok's tail over my legs.

And then sleep took me all the way down.

I stirred, totally enmeshed with Taliok in the morning. I'd pressed even closer to him in my sleep, my forehead against his chest, one of my thighs stuck between his. In my grogginess, I shifted, feeling the jut of his erection against my hip. Not completely awake, I sighed, sleepy arousal filling my core. I moved slightly, angling my hips so that Taliok's leg was pressing against my needy clit, and began contentedly rocking against him.

Taliok's warm hands drifted against my back, my sides, growing harder and needier.

"Melanie," he rasped, his breath hot against my forehead.

"Mmm?"

His speaking was starting to fully wake me up, now. And when I fully awoke, I froze. For fuck's sake. I was so into him that I was basically humping him in my sleep, now? I hadn't gotten enough last night?

Maybe it didn't matter. If I wanted him, I wanted him. Clearly, he wanted me, too...

But then I heard voices outside. Very close, as clear as the sunlight coming in through the tent's gaps.

Kat and Galok.

We weren't alone. And if I could hear them that clearly, then...

Oh, man. I couldn't wait to see the look on Kat's face when I went out there.

Not.

Taliok didn't seem to care about the others just outside our tent. He groaned then nuzzled against my ear, pressing his cock against my stomach. For a moment, I wanted to give in, say fuck it all, and climb right on top of him again. But the sharp quip of Kat saying something to Galok outside brought me back to reality.

"Come on. It's morning. We should get up."

I wrestled away from Taliok's tail and limbs, not necessarily an easy feat. But reluctantly, he let me go. He sat up, his elbows on his knees, watching me as I dressed. I had to keep my eyes away from him. Because they kept going straight to that extremely impressive, rock-hard cock.

"You should get ready, too," I said, doing up my pants.

"I will," he replied. But he made no move to do so. His eyes trailed over the curves of my body. I hesitated, wanting nothing more than to climb back into his lap. But we had people waiting for us and things to do.

"Alright. Come out when you're ready," I said hastily before jogging out of the tent, trying to put more space between us. Being in there with him was fucking with my head. If I stayed in there one more second, I'd probably never make it out.

As predicted, Kat was waiting for me, arms crossed. Even with her hood and sunglasses, I could see she was scowling. I strode past her, trying to look nonchalant, entering the tent I had shared with her to get my own solar protection jacket and sunglasses. She followed me, planting her hands on her hips after shoving her sunglasses up over her forehead.

"So, what the hell was that last night?"

"What was what?" I asked, trying to buy myself some time. How was I supposed to explain it to her when I could barely understand it myself? I still didn't quite know what this was with Taliok. I mean, I know he thought of me as his mate. But what was he to me?

"Don't play dumb. You and I are both way too fucking smart for that," Kat snapped, her blue eyes like sharp stars in her face. She was right. There was no reason to play games. She was my friend, and I'd just have to be honest.

"I spent the night with Taliok."

"Yeah, no shit," she shot back. "Everyone from here to Timbuktu could hear you guys."

Shit. I flushed, embarrassed.

"Sorry about that," I muttered, pulling my arms through the sleeves of my jacket.

"Oh my God, I mean, it's fine. Or whatever. But what is going on? You said nothing had happened with you guys."

"Well, I guess that's changed," I admitted with a shrug.

Things had definitely changed between Taliok and me. The question was, how much?

Kat's annoyance softened into concern, and I felt a wave of affection for her. Kat and I were both 23. I got the sense she'd had a tough life, like me. But where I coped with my past by shutting down and keeping people out, she coped with hers with brash anger. She wasn't mad at me. She was worried about me. Which I totally understood. I'd been worried about Cece and Chapman, too. But strangely, almost euphorically, I didn't feel worried about myself. But of course, Kat didn't know any of this. Hence her very loud and aggressive concern.

"I know you're worried about me," I said. "I would be, too. But try to believe me when I say I think this is a good thing. Taliok... I trust him." As the words came out of my mouth, I knew they were true. I was coming to trust an alien from another planet more than anyone from my own family, more than anyone from my old life.

Kat narrowed her eyes, then sighed.

"Fine," she huffed. "I trust you. You've got a good head on your shoulders. But you tell Taliok that he makes one wrong move and he'll have one more scar to add to his collection – one where his balls used to be."

I burst out laughing at my tiny fighter of a friend. But I sobered when she did not join me. She was totally serious.

"I don't think that will be needed, but thanks."

Kat paused then asked, "So, does this mean you'll be sharing a tent with him for the rest of the trip?"

I hadn't thought about it But thinking about it now, I knew that I wanted to. Even now, I was wondering what Taliok was doing in his tent. Even now, I wanted to be with him again.

But I also didn't want to abandon Kat halfway through our trip.

"Not if you don't want me to," I said, but she shook her head.

"Nah. I sleep better alone, anyway. Go be barf-worthy with your mate, it's fine."

Your mate. Something about those words sounded really good. Was it the "your" that acknowledged Taliok as mine? Or was it the "mate" part? Did I want to fully commit to this, to be his mate? That was different than a boyfriend, even a husband. It was a soulmate, a forever bond. Was I ready for that? With Taliok?

I stepped out of the tent, followed by Kat, still mulling over my questions.

Outside, Galok was preparing his irkdu for the rest of the ride. Taliok was deconstructing his tent, his hands moving quickly. I licked my lips as I watched his fingers working deftly. Fingers that had felt so good last night...

"You gonna eat?" Kat's voice cut in sharply. She was holding out some strips of dried meat and a valok plant. I took them from her. After last night's exertions, I would need to replenish my strength.

Soon we were all ready to go. Kat mounted the irkdu, with Galok's help, I noticed, then Taliok in turn boosted me up. A half a moment later, he was behind me settling in closer than he had in previous days. As we began moving, completing the last leg of the journey, I was more aware of Taliok than ever. His body was a wall of fire at my back. More than once, I shifted on the saddle and felt a corresponding pang between my legs. God, I was turned on just from him sitting behind me.

The huge rock formations all around us grew and grew as we journeyed forward, Taliok's people's mountains coming into clearer view. The closer we got, the more impressive they became – huge jagged peaks piercing the sky, much higher than the cliffs we had seen thus far. And the stone was darker, too. Blood red where so much of the desert was a coppery-gold.

As the mountain range grew and then closed around us, Kat whistled.

"Nice digs, Gahn Taliok!" she called over from Galok's irkdu, grinning beneath her sunglasses.

Galok looked over, raising the spear he held in agreement.

"I have never been in your territory, Gahn Taliok. It is truly impressive."

Taliok grunted to them. Then, soft words against my hood.

"What do you think of my mountains, Melanie from beyond the stars?"

I arched back slightly, resting my shoulders against his front and enjoying the tensing of his muscles I felt as I did so.

"I love them," I said honestly. I leaned back even more, relaxing against Taliok's front, tilting my head back to look up at the glorious peaks around us. But the sound of warriors calling and more irkdu made me snap to attention, my gaze thrusting forward.

Six men on irkdu were coming towards us in the valley we occupied. My heart hammered, instantly on alert, but Taliok raised his curved weapon in greeting. As they got closer, they raised their tails to Taliok, and I relaxed. *These must be Taliok's men.*

"Gahn Taliok," called a warrior from the front of the group. "We have no news to report since you were here last. Everything continues as it once has. Hunting has been plentiful."

"Good," Taliok said. His chest rumbled against my back as he spoke. "These women are Melanie and Kat from the new tribe. This man is Galok, from Gahn Buroudei's tribe." Taliok's warriors tensed, their eyes shifting to Galok. "He has been a good friend and ally on this trip," Taliok added, and the tension eased.

"I am glad to be here and see your mountains," Galok called over easily.

"Same!" threw in Kat.

And with that, a certain ease descended.

"We will continue with our patrols, Gahn, and will hunt more for you and your party," said the warrior.

Taliok's tail swished, and his men dispersed, leaving us alone again.

After they'd gone, I mulled over what Taliok had said. How he'd introduced me.

"Why didn't you tell them who I was?"

I felt Taliok's gaze on the back of my hood, but I couldn't turn around and face him. It was too humiliating. I couldn't believe I'd even asked that in the first place. What had I wanted, for Taliok to hold me above his head and scream that I was his mate, his Gahnala? I hadn't even told him I wanted to be his mate, for God's sake. I was being stupid.

"Nevermind," I said quickly. "Please just forget I asked that."

Taliok was silent for a moment, then grumbled, "As you wish."

Taliok urged his mount forward, leading the way through this area of the mountains. We followed the curve of the huge peak on our right around to where the ground sloped downward, ending in a flat round area that felt secluded and sheltered.

"When my people all lived here, this is where our tents stood," Taliok said.

I cast my eyes over the flat clearing. It made sense. It was a small, safe spot, closed in by the mountains. The ground was low and flat, hard and cracked. It almost looked like there could have been a lake here at some point, thousands of years ago. Across the round plain, I noticed a few remaining tents, and what looked like a fire pit. The guards' living area.

We were well into the day, now, the sun high and gleaming on the red stone. Taliok and Galok both dismounted, helping Kat and me down.

Kat whistled again, and I glanced her way.

"Everything you hoped for?" I asked.

"Honestly, no idea. I had no clue what to expect, but this is damn cool."

She took off walking across the plain, and I followed, paying close attention to the ground beneath my feet, the pebbles I saw. Many of them gleamed red and copper, but there were other colours, too – black and grey and even some white. I crouched, picking up a chalky white rock, studying it closely. Zinc and titanium dioxide from earth were found in other minerals, but they had a white cast. *I wonder if this could be useful for our sunscreen...*

A shadow fell over the rock in my hand, extending beyond my head. A huge shadow. A hulking, lurking shadow.

I stood, tucking the white pebble into my pocket.

"Did you find something of interest?" Taliok asked.

"Maybe," I said. "But we'll need to explore more. There's a lot to look at!" I was starting to feel excited. This was an opportunity I had never dreamed of on Earth – travelling to another planet and studying the natural formations there. It was crazy. And I was looking forward to digging into it.

"That is good. There are many treasures in these mountains. For example, we have much ablik."

My eyes fell to the huge black blade he still held at the ready in his hand. For such a warlike people, having access to the materials that made such strong weapons would definitely be a big advantage.

Kat and I continued wandering the perimeter of the sheltered plains, taking notes of what we found for the rest of the afternoon. But even after hours of exploring and collecting dozens of potentially useful samples, I knew we'd barely scratched the surface of what these mountains had to offer. And it wouldn't be until we got some of this stuff back to one of the labs on the ship that we'd know if we'd found anything useful. But still, it was exhilarating. And it wasn't just different rocks and minerals we were encountering, but plants, too, such as larger versions of the strange babkit trees that grew sparsely in the other territories. They had brownish trunks, but no green leaves to speak of. Instead, the brown material of their branches flattened into broad paddles that faced the sun. There were the lovely rindla flowers I'd seen in Gahn Fallo's hills, but they grew in different colours here – shocking orange and dusty pink. There were also viny plants I hadn't seen before – long dark cords with spiky black leaves that climbed up the lower boulders and ridges of the mountains and curled around the babkit tree trunks.

The entire time we worked, Galok and Taliok trailed behind us, keeping watch. I was constantly aware of Taliok's presence, his position in relation to mine. And even though I was enjoying exploring this place so much, when Taliok's hunters returned and started building the evening fire for dinner, I was glad to stop and sit and eat, just so I could be near Taliok in the darkness again.

At the evening fire, I kept shifting closer and closer to Taliok until my knee was pressed against his thigh. His men brought him the choicest bits of meat, which he, in turn, offered to me first. As we ate, the sun descended behind the mountains, casting a gold sheen on top of the arching stone. The sky morphed, the colours changing every moment – brilliant tourmaline, pink opal and pearl, cobalt blue. Once the sun disappeared and its light began to fade, the mountains turned into stark indigo silhouettes against the diamond-pricked backdrop of the sky. Then the asteroid ring rose, making everything glow.

It was an undeniably romantic scene. The murmurs of the others talking fell away until it felt like I was just Taliok and me, looking at the stars. Well, I was looking at the stars. He was looking at me.

I turned and caught his gaze, sinking into his sight stars, so sharp and silver in the darkness instead of the usual warm gold. Being here with him, it all just felt... Right. And for the first time, I got a sense of just how much he'd sacrificed to be near me. This place was beyond breathtaking. It was his home. His people's land. And he'd left it behind, moving away from his territory, something that went totally against his nature, just so he could be with me.

And I hadn't even agreed to fully be with him yet.

The deep generosity and devotion of this alien warrior, this man, flooded through me, heating me from the inside. Feeling almost drunk on the feeling, I leaned towards him, revelling in his scent.

"I'm done eating. Let's go to your tent."

Taliok did not hesitate. He rose immediately, then held out his hand, helping me to my feet.

"We are leaving," he announced to the others, his voice sounding clipped. Kat snorted, Galok grinned, and the other men raised their tails.

"Come on," I whispered, giving his huge warm hand a gentle tug. And together we walked to his tent, the fire flickering behind us, and the glow of the stars lighting the way ahead.

20

TALIOK

Melanie had joined me in my tent for the second night in a row. I was truly the luckiest Gahn to walk the Sea Sands. Some may have said that Gahns Buroudei and Fallo were luckier, as they had mates who had fully accepted them, and laid with them every night. But those Gahns did not have Melanie for their mate. Therefore, they could not be the luckiest. Only I was.

In the thick darkness of my tent, I loomed behind her, like one of my mountains casting a long shadow over a flower. I heard her breath catch at my nearness. My cock stirred, and I reached up, brushing her dark locks away from her neck. I pressed my face against the smooth column of her throat, and her head rolled back against me.

"This place is so beautiful," she murmured as I dragged my nose up and down the side of her neck, letting her scent overwhelm me. My cock was more than stirring, now. It was pulsing. Aching.

"It is," I agreed. "But it is far more beautiful with you in it." The words were true. Seeing Melanie among my mountains, in the land of my people, awoke something primal inside me.

It was perfection made real. Like everything I could have hoped for, everything that should be, was falling into place. She sighed as my lips brushed her skin, and she unzipped the front of her stiff cloak, quickly slipping it off and letting it fall to a heap. She pressed back into me and I groaned, my hands gripping her shoulders.

"It must have been hard to leave it," she said. At first, I did not know what she meant. I was too lost in her scent, her beauty, her body. I'd lost track of the conversation. But then I realized. *She means here. The mountains.*

"It was no great matter knowing what awaited me at the Cliffs of Uruzai," I replied. It had not been a difficult decision to move to be with the new women at the Cliffs. There had not been any decision at all. There had been no choice. I had to be with her. There was no other way.

"But still," she breathed, angling her head to give me better access. I nipped gently at her skin, my cock throbbing at the quiver I felt run through her in response. "Still. You've sacrificed a lot to be with me already. I just want you to know I appreciate it."

I stopped, my hands growing hard against her skin. She truly did not understand this bond, or me. She did not understand the depth of my love for her. That life in the mountains without her was no life at all.

Gripping her shoulders, I spun her around to face me, catching her delicate chin between my fingers.

"I would do anything for you," I hissed. Even in the darkness, I could see her eyes widen. I sounded aggressive, crazed, even. But she needed to understand the depth of this. The ferocity of my love for her. "My love for you is unending. It guides me in everything I do. Of course, I moved to the Cliffs of Uruzai in the hopes that you would accept me as your mate. But I am a patient Gahn. And so is my love. It will wait for you, for whenever you decide to be with me. But I could not have waited here, in my mountains, so far from you. I did not have to make a choice. There was no choice."

No, there was no choice. Only fate.

Melanie stared at me, her breath shaky and shallow.

"And what happens if you wait for me, you wait all that time, and I never agree to be your mate?"

I tensed. My tail jerked. Dread formed a large stone in my guts, but I breathed around it. I knew this could be a possibility. I knew as soon as I found out she did not feel the mate bond as I did that she might not choose me.

I slipped my fingers from her chin, gliding them across the smooth swell of her cheekbone. Her eyes fluttered closed, and she leaned into my hand. My chest clenched.

"If you never agree to be my mate, my love will still be there, all the same. I will wait for you forever. Even if you never choose me, even if all that waiting was for nothing, it would still have been worth it in the end."

My hand tightened against her face, and my other hand moved up to join it, pinning her jaw and tilting her head back, gently. She cracked her eyes open to look at me, chest heaving.

"It still would have been worth it," I ground out, "Because the act of loving you has been, and will always be, the greatest honour of my life."

Melanie gasped, and a single bead of liquid escaped from one eye. I halted its path with my thumb and bent my face closer to hers.

"Taliok?" My name was a stir of breath against my mouth.

"Yes?"

"*Kiss* me."

"I will do anything you ask, Melanie. But I do not know this word from your world. This *kiss*."

Her breath huffed. She arched, her breasts pressing against my chest, making my head fog over with desire.

168

"Put your mouth on mine," she said thickly, hurriedly. And like the devoted Gahn I was, I obeyed.

Her mouth was sweet, wet, and waiting. It opened for me immediately, allowing me instant access. I took full advantage, swiping inside, tasting, invading with my tongues. Melanie's palms slid up my chest to my neck, then back through my hair. The sensations coalesced, moving down my neck, down my body, into my cock.

After a few breathless, moments she pulled away, panting.

"Lie down," she said. "It's time for your next lesson. And take off your loincloth."

I did so, my eyes never leaving her. As I'd promised her before, I removed my weapons, too, so that I was totally bare before her. Her mouth fell open as she took me in with her eyes.

"Lie down," she said again, more huskily this time. I did so, my eyes hooding as I kept her in my gaze.

She stripped quickly until she was as bare as me. I cursed myself for not having had the foresight to have lit a valok candle so that I could see her beauty more easily. But when her wet mouth descended onto my cock, all thoughts of candles fell away. In fact, all thoughts completely escaped my head. The only thing left was Melanie and the hot pleasure of her mouth on my cock.

Unable to help myself, my hips lifted from the ground, and my hands fisted in her hair. I did not know that this was done between mates. I did not know something could feel this good.

Melanie released my cock and then stroked it with her hand.

"This is called a *blow job*," she breathed against my skin. I bucked up, hoping to find her mouth once more. With a soft moan, she guided my swollen head back to her mouth, beginning to suck and working my shaft with her hand as she did so. I growled, my hips leaping, when her other hand gently traced the sensitive skin at my balls. The sensations were overwhelming.

Too overwhelming. I was going to reach the peak of my pleasure far too soon. I did not want to do so, not yet. I needed more of her first.

"Melanie." I barely got it out. My voice sounded broken.

"Mmph," she said around my cock, the vibration of her voice sending a shiver through my skin. I hooked a claw under her chin, guiding her up and off of me. My cock slipped from her mouth with a slick pop.

I kept one claw under her chin, applying subtle pressure, drawing her forward. She crawled over me, her nipples dragging across my skin, her thighs on either side of me. I wasn't even sure what I was doing or where I wanted her to go, but this image – Melanie crawling on me, over me, her eyes glazed, her mouth wet and open, was one I'd remember forever. It almost made me spill my seed right there.

When she reached my chest, her legs splayed over my ribs, her breasts pressing into my skin, I realized exactly where I needed her to be. But first, another *kiss*.

I drew her chin further forward. She gave a soft groan as she moved in, pressing her lips to mine. My hips arched up against nothing as the sensations of her mouth echoed all the way down my body. She began to grind on my skin, her wetness a hot slick on my chest.

"Not like this," I grunted. I gripped her hips, lifting her easily. She yelped as I settled her directly on my face. I held her hips in place. And held them hard.

At first, I did nothing but breathe the scent of her in. It rammed through my body, slamming me with desire. The scent was so sweet, so arousing. I could no longer hold back. With a low groan, I released my tongues from behind my fangs and feasted.

Melanie jerked sharply, her hands falling to mine on her hips.

"Taliok," she moaned. I could feel her muscles quivering on either side of my face. Every time I experienced something new with Melanie, I thought it was the greatest joy possible. But then something else happened that was even better. But certainly, this must be the best. Having my face thrust between her trembling white thighs as she moaned.

Her hands were squeezing my fingers at her hips, clutching for purchase, as if trying to tether herself to something of this world. I slicked my three tongues through her folds, lapping up all the wetness I found there and thanking my great luck when even more wetness appeared. This was the finest sensation of my warrior's life. A luxury I had never imagined to exist.

On one track back down through her folds, my strong centre tongue caught in something open and warm. I pressed inward, and her body welcomed me greedily. *Her cunt.* My tongue was inside her cunt. My cock pulsed, and I pulled one hand free from Melanie's grip to squeeze my shaft, trying to regain some sense of control. But it was difficult. Impossible. Because my tongue was pressing ever inward, sucked into wanting heat. I slipped my tongue out, then back in, then repeated that motion, thrusting upward into her cunt. Melanie moaned over and over, dropping her hips even lower, grinding her *clit* against my nose, riding my tongue. I stared up at her, entranced, watching the softness of her stomach and breasts shake with her movements. Then she arched, and everything in her tightened. My tongue was caught in a vise of pleasure as she came, rocking against my face, her hands grappling at the top of my head for purchase, tangling in my hair.

I could not wait. Could no longer control myself. With Melanie coming on my tongue, I gripped my cock, jerking it hard and fast and rough. Ragged. Feral. I left my tongue buried in her while continuing to probe and taste her with my other two tongues. I imagined being buried this deep with my cock instead of my tongue, and that sent me over the edge. Seed spilled and spilled. I felt my eyes roll back in my head as I gave in to the sensations: Melanie's scent, wetness, and skin all over my face and tongue and my hand pulling at my cock. I exploded again even after the initial spill of seed, and I kept stroking myself through it, tugging the last strokes of pleasure from my body.

Melanie was hunched over my face, still holding the top of my head. Reluctantly, I slipped my tongue out of her. She made a small sound of protest, and I eagerly moved to insert my tongue again, but she said, "*Holy crap*, no. I can't do any more."

She swung her leg over my head, shuffling downward and collapsing against my side, breathing hard.

"That was incredible," she whispered, nuzzling into me. I turned onto my side, pulling her harder against me, running my hand down her back.

"You are incredible," I murmured against the top of her head. And she was. She was from another world, more perfect than anything here. Incredible. Impossible to believe. A wonder among wonders.

As Melanie sighed contentedly and brushed her nose against my chest, relaxing into sleep, I suddenly remembered Gahn Buroudei's words. When he'd been advising me on how to win my human mate to me, he'd said, "Tongues, Taliok. Tongues." Perhaps he had not been playing me for a fool after all. *Buroudei is a wise Gahn indeed*, I thought soberly. I was wrong to be angry at advice that had turned out to be so good. He and Zeezee both had helped me get here. I was grateful to them. And I was so grateful for every scrap of joy

Melanie offered me. I would take it all, and I'd drink it down the way I had sucked at the wetness of her cunt.

My spent cock stirred again at the memory, and I palmed it, stifling a growl. Melanie was breathing softly, already asleep. I needed to sleep, too. She had taken much of my strength, and much of my seed. Rest was important.

For a creature so small, this human woman had astonishing power. And I would happily raise my tail before that power, every day, for the rest of my days.

If she'll have me.

I pushed that thread of doubt away. Yes, I had not fully mated Melanie, and she had not fully accepted me. But every day, we got closer. The bond between us was growing, and soon it would be a sacred mate bond for her as much as it was for me. I was sure of it. We had already come so far.

Besides, I'd spoken true earlier. I would wait for her forever. Even if she never chose me.

Even if she never loved me.

But I hoped... I hoped, that she would.

I hoped.

And I hungered.

21

MELANIE

I stretched as I woke up, my body feeling weak in the best possible way. And warm in the best possible way, with Taliok's huge frame cocooning mine. His massive arm was slung over my torso, drawing my back against his strong chest. I breathed in and out, slowly, just allowing myself to feel this moment. The peace of it. The comfort.

I could get used to waking up like this, I thought.

I could get used to waking up like this every fucking day.

Especially if every night was like last night.

Flashes hit me, over and over. Taliok's hardness in my mouth. Then his tongue, deep inside me, turning me inside out with pleasure. No wonder I felt so weak. That had been an Olympic-level orgasm.

Imagine what it will be like when he fucks you.

My cheeks heated at that unbidden thought. Every day I was inching closer towards actually having penetrative sex with Taliok. I was getting closer to mating with him. I couldn't deny that last night, when I'd been grinding against his face, the thing that had gotten me off wasn't just the physical feeling of it, but the idea of being penetrated by Taliok. I wanted his hardness inside me. I wanted him to come deep in my pussy. But did I want everything that came along with that? The commitment?

I mean, waking up with him like this every day sounded pretty damn good. The more time I spent with Taliok, the more time I wanted to spend with him. I wiggled, nuzzling further back against his body, feeling a small thrill when his arm tightened. As if to keep me here with him. As if to keep me safe.

I didn't want this feeling to end.

It doesn't have to.

I could accept him as my mate. I could just go for this, headfirst. All in. Never look back.

I tilted my head back, taking in his sleeping face. In sleep, he didn't have the usual tense seriousness in his expression. Everything was smoothed out and softened. He looked so much younger like this. I could almost picture him as the boy he'd been before he'd gotten his scars.

Affection rushed through me so hard it stole my breath and made my ribs ache. No, there wouldn't be any escaping this, now. There wouldn't be any denying it.

The fact of the fucking matter was that I was falling in love with Taliok. Head over heels, for this brooding alien warrior.

Admitting it to myself was a relief. I wasn't going to hide from it anymore, and I wasn't going to push him away. I would do this, with him. The man I'd come to trust, and come to love, over the time we'd spent together. And now that I'd made my decision, I couldn't wait to jump in.

I turned over in his arms, running my hands down his neck to his chest. I moved my lips to his face, kissing each deep scar, each inch of torn flesh. Taliok cracked open a black and gold eye, his sight stars contracting as they focused on my face.

"Good morning," I breathed, almost giddy. I couldn't wait to see his reaction to what I had to tell him. That I was in love with him. That I was willing to give this whole mate thing a try. "I have something to tell you."

"Oh?" he asked, before pressing his own lips to my forehead, I let my eyes flutter closed, tilting my head up against the feeling of his kiss. Before I knew it his mouth met mine, lips pressing, opening, urging. I moaned into his mouth, parting my thighs...

"Rise and shine, sleepyheads! We ever gonna get our shit started or what?"

Kat's loud voice boomed through the fabric of the tent. I jumped, and Taliok's arms tightened around me, a growl building in his throat. I took a few calming breaths, willing my heart to slow down now that I knew it was just Kat being her usual loud self outside. But clearly, she was waiting for me, and I didn't think she was going to give up on this little tirade.

"Let's pick this back up later," I said, my voice serious, staring into Taliok's eyes.

"Nothing could keep me away," he replied, just as serious. *Good grief.* These guys really just said whatever deep, dramatic thing came into their heads. On anyone else, it would seem cheesy, even kind of stupid. But Taliok made everything sound like a dream. He was a man of deep, awe-inspiring, always serious, always sincere words. And it turned out I fucking loved him for it.

I pressed one more quick kiss to his lips, wanting to do so, *so* much more than that, before I wriggled backwards out of his arms. I started to dress, and he watched me with relentless eyes as I did so. I slapped my sunscreen on, grabbed my sunglasses, then jogged outside to meet Kat. Any longer in that confined space with Taliok and I'd be tearing off the clothes I'd just put on.

Kat nodded at me as I emerged,

"I thought I was going to have to come in there and drag you out," she muttered with a wry grin. I shook my head. I may have become a besotted idiot much faster than I would have thought possible, but I knew we still had work to do. We'd come here for a reason, after all.

The rustle of fabric behind me let me know Taliok had emerged. I felt him at my back a split second later. I turned my head back, admiring him in the bright light of day.

He held out dried meat and valok for our breakfast.

"Thanks," I said. I turned to Kat.

"I already ate," she said. "Mr. Friendly over there wouldn't leave me alone until I did. Something about being so small and putting some meat on my bones. Yadda yadda."

She jerked her thumb over her shoulder at Galok who hovered nearby. He grinned, then raised his tail at the sight of me, and I gave him a wave before digging into my breakfast. When I was done, Kat and I got to work, followed by Taliok and Galok. Taliok's guard party, whom I'd seen briefly in the encampment, dispersed for their patrolling and hunting duties.

Kat and I had already picked over a large portion of the plains area where the tents were located, and Taliok led us through a long crevice into another rockier, smaller valley beyond the tents. The blood-red mountains rose up jaggedly around us, and we had to really watch our feet on the boulders. Taliok kept a sturdy hand on my elbow, which I was thankful for. He and Galok had no trouble traversing the boulders and stones with their long and wide clawed feet. But for Kat and I, it was much more treacherous, our stiff boots slipping in the dust. More than once, Galok's long arms shot out to steady Kat when she stumbled, which always earned him some kind of burning remark. But her remarks bounced off him like a goddamn trampoline. An old saying from my childhood came to me. *I'm rubber, you're glue....*

Eventually, we made it to a flatter area in the valley where we could walk mostly unhindered.

"This can be our home base for the day," I said to Kat, dumping my pack on the ground. She did the same before straightening and looking around, hands on her hips.

"Yeah, sounds good. Looks like a great spot."

Did it ever. The gorgeous variety of rocks and minerals present in these mountains was overwhelming. Our packs were already heavy with numerous samples, and there I was eyeing a bunch more stuff that I wanted to take back with us.

Kat and I got to work, crouching and examining, dusting off and collecting. I was constantly aware of Taliok nearby. He did his best, it seemed, not to hover and stare, giving me some space to work. But I almost wished he would hover. My eyes kept flicking to him, wishing he were closer.

After a while, I noticed Taliok wasn't just hanging around doing nothing. He, too, seemed to be collecting rock samples. Every once in a while when I'd look over, I'd see him crouching, scarred brow furrowed, staring at a shining pebble or bit of rock. Sometimes he tossed his rock away, but other times he placed it in the rounded shadow of a nearby boulder. The next time I looked over, I saw his collection had grown into a little pile.

"I'll be right back," I called to Kat, who was working about fifteen feet away from me. She waved me off, then turned that dismissive wave to Galok, who was leaning over her shoulder trying to see what she was doing.

I stood, dusting off my pants, then walked over to Taliok.

He must have heard me coming, or smelled me, or something, because his ears pricked, and his eyes snapped to me immediately. He stepped up between his little rock pile and me as if trying to hide it.

"What are you doing?" I asked, leaning around him to see.

Wow. It looked like he'd collected the most stunning rocks he could find. Deep red, smoky grey, shimmering orange, and glassy pink. He grunted, looking over his shoulder at the pile and then back at me.

"I promised never to deceive you, so I will tell it to you true," he said slowly. My heart sank. Oh no. What had he wanted to hide from me? Was the illusion of the perfect Taliok about to get shattered? I steeled myself, mouth dry.

"I am collecting stones for your Gahnala-Kai Rek."

I blinked.

Gahnala-Kai Rek. The alien wedding ring thing?

"Gahn Irokai collected the decorations for Exoka's Gahnala-Kai Rek from these mountains himself," Taliok continued. "And I vowed to do the same." He watched me with sharp eyes, then added quickly, "I do not mean to pressure you. I make no presumptions. And perhaps I do this out of a foolish kind of hope, but…" Once again he looked back at his little pile of rocks, and I wanted to fucking scream. He was so pure, so ardent. It was breaking my heart and putting it back together at the same time. My eyes pricked with tears.

He spoke again, softly, his eyes still trained on the stones but seeming far away. "I have never been one for optimism. Never been one for hope." Those golden eyes shifted back to me, making me suck in a sharp breath. "But that seems to have changed."

I couldn't speak. My throat was constricting in on itself. I blinked hard, overwhelmed by him, by this. But overwhelmed in the best possible way.

I felt my face break open into the widest, tear-stained

smile. Taliok's tail jerked, his sight stars pulsing. He stepped up to me, drawing his knuckles gently across my cheekbone.

"I have never seen you smile like this. So wide." His voice got lower, rasping, "It is very beautiful."

I let out a shaky laugh, swiping at my eyes beneath my sunglasses.

"You're one to talk," I said. "I don't think I've ever seen you smile."

Taliok leaned closer, drawing his knuckles down to my lower lip. He wasn't exactly smiling, but his mouth had kind of... Softened upward.

"When my father died," he said, "I think that I forgot how. And when Gahn Irokai was killed, the memory was buried deeper. But you, Melanie from beyond the stars, are reminding just what it is to smile again."

His mouth shifted further upward until it became the shadow of a smile. It was just a shadow, and the scarred side of his face was tighter than the other, but it was still fucking breathtaking.

You need to tell him. Tell him now.

No more waiting. It was time to tell Taliok I loved him. That I would do this with him. Be his mate, his Gahnala, and wear the beautiful stones he'd chosen for me with pride. Heart pounding, ready to say the words that would change my world forever, I took a huge breath.

"Taliok, I-"

A spear whistled passed Taliok's head. If his one ear hadn't been so bent with its scarring, it would have been torn clean off.

What the fuck? What the -

I didn't even have time to finish that thought. Taliok's shadowy smile disappeared, his face twisting and turning hard. He drew a blade from his back, snarling, as he reached for me. He pressed me behind his huge frame with an arm of iron. I clutched at the straps on his back, panting and terrified. Not terrified for myself. But for Taliok.

"Galok!" Taliok warned, his voice travelling across the valley.

From around Taliok's back, I could see that Galok was already aware of what was happening. He drew a blade and then scooped Kat up with one arm, tossing her over his shoulder and loping across the valley towards the other side, the side furthest from the tents and where the spear had seemingly come from. Taliok's arm was tightening on me. He was getting ready to do the same thing – to carry me away to safety.

No. I don't want to leave you here, I screamed inside my head. *No!*

But Taliok didn't have time to follow Galok. Another spear flashed, this time with much deadlier aim. He knocked it aside with his huge curved blade, but another quickly followed. He began backing up, still clutching at me behind his back. Tears streaming, I moved backward with him, trying to make this easier for him, trying not to trip or stumble.

We backed up to a spot where a large, flat boulder rested on an angle against the side of the mountain, creating a small triangle of shadowed space, almost like a little rock tent. Taliok turned abruptly and trundled me into the small space.

"Stay here," he hissed, his tone commanding, his face a dark mask. My eyes wide, my throat tight, I could only nod and watch as he sprinted back the way we'd come towards whatever threat was waiting. Moments later, I saw Galok running in the same direction, blades drawn and ready.

A heartbeat passed. Then two. Then three. And I began to sob.

I never told him. I never told him I loved him...

If he dies now, without knowing that I love him, I'll never forgive myself.

No. No way. He won't die.

It was unfathomable. Taliok, so strong and sturdy and steady, a fucking stone wall of a warrior. He couldn't die. He just... Couldn't.

After a few hours that were probably actually only minutes, I couldn't take it anymore. I knew I shouldn't leave this sheltered spot, but I had to poke my head out. My streaming eyes scanned the area frantically, searching for any sign of my warrior, my Taliok. My mate.

But there was none. He'd gone to meet the aggressors where they stood, which wasn't here. It must have been further down the valley, in the crevice, or beyond it, at the tents...

Who would attack him here?

Gahn Buroudei and Gahn Fallo were allies. Begrudging allies, in Fallo's case, but I was sure his men wouldn't have reason to come and attack here. No way Gahn Fallo would risk his connection to us human women. Chapman would never forgive him. No, it had to be someone else. There were two other tribes of the Sea Sands, ones I had never seen or encountered...

It must be one of them, I thought, my stomach twisting in knots. I knew Taliok was so strong – a brutal warrior. But what if these men were stronger? What if he was outnumbered?

The thought was a terrible one. It felt like it was opening up a big huge valley in my chest, as red and craggy as these mountains. But painful, and pulsing with lovesick human blood.

I can't lose him.

There had to be something, *anything* I could do. I scanned the area again. There was no sign of Kat anywhere. Galok must have stashed her away somewhere safe. For now, it looked like I was on my own.

My eyes moved back to the crevice we'd come through, a narrow space that opened up into this valley on one side, and opened onto the plain with the tents on the other. *Maybe I could block it off. Or set a trap?*

My eyes moved upward, up the steep incline of the rock on either side of the crevice. In the crevice itself, the walls were a sheer perpendicular drop to the ground. But from this side, in the valley, they were slightly less steep. And about twenty feet up, there was a small ledge. A ledge with a precarious-looking boulder right at the edge.

A scenario unfolded in my head, cartoon-like, like something out of the Roadrunner.

I could climb up there and watch what was happening below. If it looked like an enemy was making his way through the crevice, coming this way, I could try to take him out by pushing the boulder down.

It was risky as all get out. But I couldn't sit here and do nothing while my mate fought this battle alone. I was going to be his Gahnala, his queen. I had to fucking act like one.

One more quick glance told me that now was as good as ever. If I waited too long, I might miss my chance, and I could be spotted by someone coming my way. I crouched, touching my fingers to the dusty rock, then bolted. I tried to stay low, like I'd seen people do in action movies, but it slowed me down too much. Adrenaline took over, making me sprint across the treacherous land. I'd never been much of a runner, but stress was a hell of a performance enhancer, and I made it over to the slope I hoped to climb pretty damn fast.

I had to stop for a second at the bottom of the slope to catch my breath, my heart pounding so hard I swore it would break my ribs. This planet had slightly less oxygen than Earth, and my body was definitely feeling the effects.

But I had to keep going.

I was desperately aware of time passing. Time that Taliok could be getting hurt or that his enemies could be advancing this way.

Panting hard and gritting my teeth, I started to climb.

22

TALIOK

I ran from the valley, legs pumping over the uneven stones, blades in my claws to face my foes. Behind me, I could hear Galok catching up. His legs were longer than mine, and he moved quickly. A moment later he was at my side.

"These are not Gahn Buroudei's men, I am sure," he said as he leapt over a boulder in his path.

"I know," I grunted. "They are Gahn Baldor's men." Gahn Baldor's tribal territory was closest to mine, between the mountains and the bitter sea beyond.

"How many do you think there are?" Galok said.

I did not respond. There was no way to know. Gahn Baldor had a large tribe. But so far only a few spears had been thrown. I dodged another as it whirred past my head.

As the crevice widened to meet the plains, we found them, blades drawn. Five men. My own men were still out in their various duties, hunting and patrolling. They were good guards, but our land was vast. Gahn Baldor's men had slipped through. *My men could be far from here now, and may not scent our enemies nor hear the sounds of the battle.* I could not count on them to return. But the rage that filled me with dark smoke told me that I would not need them. Any man who threatened my territory while my mate was in it would die.

I ran up the craggy side of the sloping rock wall beside me then leapt, Irokai's old blade held high, smashing it down on the first opponent. It cracked easily through the bone handle of the spear he held, and before he could recover, I sliced his arm from his body. He kept fighting, though, with his remaining arm, and was soon joined by a second warrior.

I snapped my jaws, moving my large curved blade to one hand and drawing a second long knife with my other, fighting both men off at once. In the side of my vision, I could see Galok fighting two men, too.

But there had been five men.

Where is the fifth warrior?

I grunted, my arms wheeling, weapons clanging against my enemies. The man whom I had injured was slowing down as he bled out, but between the two of them, I was too distracted to try to locate the missing fifth man.

But then, between flashing blades, I saw him – a dark streak among all the red rock. He was running down the length of the crevice, straight for the valley. Straight for where I'd left Melanie.

No!

A new strength exploded in me, lighting up my veins. I had never roared in battle like other men did, but in that moment, I could not stop the guttural, raging sound tearing from my throat. My arms moved faster than they ever had. The wounded man fell, leaving me only one opponent. Snarling like a beast, I hefted my blades against him, over and over again, driving him back until his spine hit stone. As he tried to duck out of the trap, I arched my curved blade up from below, drawing it hard against his neck. He, too, fell quickly, and I spun, locating Galok. I lifted my shorter knife and hurled it, the black blade spinning through the air and landing in the back of one of Galok's opponents. That man fell, and Galok focused on the fourth man, leaving me to track down the fifth. At that moment, the sound of men calling and irkdu rushing caught my ears, and I whipped around to see three of my warriors racing towards us over the plain.

"Secure our territory! Track down any others and kill them!" I shouted as I turned, already starting to run. I flew over the rocks and boulders, knowing each of their hard forms from birth. They did not hinder me. I leapt and crouched and rolled and landed, sprinting for the valley. For the fifth man.

For my mate.

I did not stop at the mouth of the valley. I sped forward, right for the spot I had left Melanie. My heart was a war drum, a thundering storm, a plea. A plea for her to still be there. To be unharmed.

I skidded to a stop, my claws raking into the boulder that laid against the rock.

Melanie was not there.

23

MELANIE

I was only halfway up this freaking hill, and my body was already close to giving out. Although, to be fair, it wasn't much of a hill, now. More like a treacherous, steep incline with jagged rocks and slipping stones. Grunting, I reached up for a rock about the size of my head, pulling hard. I hadn't been much of an athlete back on Earth, let alone someone who was into rock climbing. It was taxing my body to the limit.

But then I thought of Taliok, fighting, maybe hurt, maybe alone, and a fresh wave of will fuelled me. I thought of Kat, too, somewhere in this valley. *If I could get to the top, to that boulder, I might actually be able to do something to help both of them. All of us.*

My palms were on fire, and it took me a while to realize I was bleeding. So many of the rocks were the colour of human blood, so I didn't take much notice of the dark streaks on their surface. I thought it was sweat. There was certainly a lot of that pouring out of me, soaking my clothes under my solar protection jacket and streaming from beneath my sunglasses. But when I stopped at a relatively stable spot and took a look at my hands, I saw that they were red and raw, cut up from the stones. *Fucking weak-ass human skin.* None of the aliens had any trouble traversing tough landscapes like this. And at that moment, I was extremely fucking jealous.

Can't stop now.

The ledge was in my sights, only about ten feet up now. Breath barely caught, I crouched back down, starting to climb again. I moved as quickly as I could, but that wasn't very fast. So many of the stones beneath my feet were loose. But I was getting so close, now. The ledge was within reach...

I stretched my hand up to it, ready to hoist myself. At that moment, my stiff boot slipped on some pebbles, and I slammed down against the rock face, hands scrabbling for purchase. My sunglasses slipped from my sweaty nose, disappearing down the rocks. I only slid down about a foot, thankfully, but it was enough to scare the ever-loving shit out of me. Not to mention I now had a bunch of bruises to go with the bleeding hands.

Then the doubt came.

Maybe I can't do this. I'm just a weak human. I'm probably going to fall to my fucking death from here. Crack my head on a stone and never be any help to anyone. And Taliok will die, and Kat and Galok, and all of this will have been for nothing.

Tears stung my eyes, and I let out a bitter cry. Everything in my life had been fucking hard. My parents, my ex-boyfriend, trying to keep myself afloat in college. Not to mention getting abducted and dumped on an alien planet. But with Taliok, things had finally seemed to be turning around. Things had been... Joyful. Loving him, it turned out, was easy. It was the easiest fucking thing I'd ever done. But now, things were going to shit. Again.

Am I cursed? Cursed to have a fucking tragedy for a life?

I was ready to give up. I almost did.

But then I heard it.

The thunder of a war cry, a roar that rattled my teeth and shot right into my bones. It echoed through the crevice and into the valley and made my chest clench.

It was Taliok.

I was sure of it.

I'd never heard him so loud. When he'd attacked Gahn Fallo, it had been silent. But now, he was screaming. Roaring. There were no words in his cry but it felt like he was calling me.

And in that moment, I knew he was doing everything possible to get back to me. Fighting tooth and claw, risking his life, plunging forward, to protect me. To come back to me.

I can't stop. I won't stop.

Tears and sweat still streaming, I wrenched my head up, focusing the ledge in my sights again, squinting without my sunglasses. And again, I started to climb. My muscles shook, my hands bled, but I forged forward, the echoes of Taliok's cry ringing out in my head and my chest and my ripped up hands. And finally, *finally*, I pulled myself up onto the ledge.

I remained on my hands and knees for a minute, head swimming. That much exertion in this atmosphere, when I wasn't even used to this kind of thing on Earth, had almost brought me to the brink. Black spots danced in front of my eyes, and I lowered my forehead to the red rock ledge, willing my blood to get back to my brain and wake the hell up.

After a few moments of kneeling, face to the rock, I felt a bit better. Not great, but enough to stand up and take stock of my surroundings. I stood carefully, not straightening all the way up, my hands on my knees.

The boulder I'd spied from the ground was directly ahead of me, and below it was the spot where the crevice opened up into the valley we'd been working in. The boulder was pretty big, coming up to my ribs. I inched up to it, gingerly placing my hands upon it, then looked down.

I could basically only see the entrance to the valley from here. The rock hill I'd been climbing continued up above me at a sharp angle, and its wall kept me from seeing much further into the crevice or onto the plain with the tents. I couldn't see Taliok. Couldn't see anyone else. But, straining my ears, I thought I could hear the echoes of blades colliding.

With such a limited view, will I even have enough warning to try to push this fucking thing down?

That question was answered almost instantly. I would not have enough warning. Because somehow, an enemy warrior had already followed me.

I heard the scrabble of claws behind me and spun, my back to the boulder. A warrior I didn't recognize, an enemy, made it to my ledge and stood before me. I cringed away. My instincts told me to move, move *back*, but I didn't think the boulder was very stable on this ledge. I was stuck, frozen in place, bleeding hands plastered to its rough face, trying not to put my weight on it though everything in my body tried to make me.

"Who are you?" The warrior's sight stars pulled into fine points. "*What* are you?" His lip pulled back from his teeth in a snarl.

"I am the Gahnala Melanie. I am Gahn Taliok's mate. And if you hurt me, he will kill you," I said shakily, trying to fortify my voice with strength.

The words felt so true. Every single one. I could only hope the last part would be true, though. I hoped Taliok was OK out there, and that he'd help me if he could. Because there was no way to help myself in this situation. I had no weapons and no way out.

"Gahn Taliok's mate? You are a female..." His eyes moved

down my body in a way that made my skin crawl. He took a step towards me, and I flinched.

"Stay the fuck back!" In my panic, I reverted to English, my native tongue. His sight stars pulsed in confusion. But still, he took another step.

A black point emerged from the front of his chest. He faltered, staring downward, his fingers rising to probe what I now realized was the tip of a spear. A spear that had gone straight through his back and out the front of his chest.

Thank you, thank you, Taliok.

He was back. He was OK. He'd come for me!

The enemy warrior fell heavily to his knees, and a moment later a knife appeared at his throat. I squeezed my eyes shut as that knife sliced, feeling sick. I opened them a moment later to see the enemy warrior's lifeless body hurtling down the rock incline, having been kicked over.

Heart pounding, I turned to face Taliok, ready to jump into his arms.

But it wasn't Taliok.

Before me stood an alien unlike any other I'd seen on this planet. He was not from the Sea Sands. I had no idea what he was.

I cringed backwards once again, mind racing, heart pounding as I stared at this new entity, this new enemy.

What fresh hell is this?

24

THE EXILE

I pulled my spear from the Sea Sand warrior's corpse and then kicked his body down the rock face before turning to the female before me. I had killed the warrior who had threatened her, but still she cowered in fear.

It is as my mother always told me, then. It is true. I am too different. My existence causes terror among others.

My eyes narrowed as I looked at the female. The being my father's people called the Kell and my mother called the Lavrika of the Bitter Seas had shown me my mate – a woman like this. And yet not like this. This woman had pale skin and dark hair that was loose and straight. The female I had seen in the sea caves of the Kell had much darker skin and she wore her hair braided like the people of the Sea Sands.

But she was not of the Sea Sands. And neither was this female.

They shared lineage, though. They were of the same tribe, I was sure.

Maybe this one will tell me where I can find her. My mate. The one with eyes like dark stars.

The female spat words I did not know at me. I had heard her speak my mother's tongue before, to the other warrior. The one I'd killed. So I spoke to her now in my mother's language, hoping she'd understand.

"I will not harm you. I wish only to ask you a question."

I had no other use for her. I would not hurt her or steal her. I wanted only to know where I could find the other one. The one who looked like her but not like her.

Her small, flat brows rose, her eyes widening. *No sight stars. How very strange.* Even I, so different from my mother's people, had sight stars. But she had none.

"What are you?" she asked in the tongue of my mother's people. The language of the Sea Sands.

I had no answer for her. I was the in-between. The exile.

I ignored her question since I had no good reply.

"Tell me where to find the other female."

Her brows furrowed.

"I don't know where Kat is, and even if I did I wouldn't tell you."

What is a Kat?

She continued, her shaking voice growing fiercer.

"My mate is Gahn Taliok. He'll be back here any minute so you'd better keep your *fucking* distance."

I regarded her, remaining still. Gahn Taliok. That must have been the scarred one. The one who followed this female everywhere. It had taken me many, many days to reach these mountains. And since I'd been here, I'd observed Gahn Taliok and his small party. Gahn Taliok and his men were of my mother's people, of the Sea Sands, but they were not of her tribe. And as I was not of the Sea Sands, and not of any tribe, I had watched them all from the shadows, never making my presence known. I had seen Gahn Baldor's men, the men of my mother's tribe, attack. And when I'd seen this female, so like the one who was meant to be my mate, cornered, I had finally revealed myself.

But now her mate returned, her Gahn Taliok. I smelled him first, his scent powerful and full of rage. I angled my head, looking down over the ledge. The one she called Gahn Taliok was running through the valley. He raced to a spot further down, bending to a boulder as if to check beneath it. Then he stood, blades thrust out at his sides, and screamed a word I did not recognize.

He will be here soon.

If he found me here with his woman, he would try to kill me. I did not doubt my strength against his. We were close to evenly matched, but I was larger, my scaled hide thicker. I would probably kill him in battle. But I did not desire to kill any more men of the Sea Sands today. They looked too much like my mother.

I returned my gaze to the frightened female before me.

"Your mate returns and you are safe. I will leave you now."

It was time to continue my journey across the Sea Sands. The search to find my mate. And I would continue that search, like I had done for so many days before, alone.

MELANIE

"Stay away from me. Stay back. Stay the fuck back!" I was babbling, stuttering. I was still speaking English as pure, visceral fear shot through my veins. The other enemy warrior had been scary, no doubt. But at least I recognized him as a species I knew and somewhat understood. He may not have been from Gahn Taliok's tribe, and he may have come here with blades drawn, but he was still somewhat familiar. But this being? This thing? He was truly a monster.

I said *he*, because one familiar thing about him was that he wore a loincloth like the Sea Sand men. There were a few other features he shared with the Sea Sand people, I realized, like his long, muscled tail, and sight stars that pulsed in large black eyes. But that was where the similarities ended. He was taller than any man of the Sea Sands, even taller than Gahn Fallo and Galok. More than eight feet tall, easily. And even outside of that insane height, he was *huge*. Where the Sea Sand warriors were intimidating aliens in their own right, this guy was a downright beast. There was something prehistoric about him. Something crocodile-like. *Crocodile? More like a dinosaur. Or dragon.* He had dark blue skin that splintered into charcoal grey scales along his shoulders and down his arms. He had no hair, but rather thick black scaly ridges that ran from his forehead down the back of his massive head and thick neck. His feet had three clawed toes like Taliok's people did, but they were larger, flatter, strangely flipper-like.

And his face. Oh fuck. There was nothing human about it. The men of the Sea Sands may have had fangs, but their jaws and smiles were vaguely human. But this creature's wide face ended in a ridged snout, grey teeth escaping from dark blue skin. He stood upright on thick, scaled legs, gripping his spear in a powerful clawed hand, his knife in the other.

But somehow, when he spoke next, I understood him. *He's speaking the language of the Sea Sands? How...?*

"I will not harm you. I wish only to ask you a question."

He spoke somewhat what strangely, as if he had some kind of accent. Or, rather than an accent, it was like his mouth wasn't built for the words he was speaking.

And those words did not put me at ease. At all. In fact, him opening his terrifying mouth made me even more afraid. Those teeth were crazy, and that jaw looked like it could snap bone like it was a tea biscuit.

But hearing him speak a language I understood helped my brain shift back into that gear, despite my fear. I was able to switch from English back to the language of the Sea Sands.

"What are you?" I asked, echoing the dead warrior's question from a few minutes ago. Seriously, what was he? The Sea Sand people were different than humans, to be sure. But they were distinctly mammalian, like us. This guy was... *reptilian.* His sight stars, a vivid sapphire blue, pulsed to a point under his heavy, scaly brow.

If he understood my question, he didn't answer it, instead asking one of his own.

"Tell me where to find the other female."

Defensive panic surged. Was he talking about Kat? Had he seen her? What did he want with her? I eyed those teeth, that massive jaw again, then let my eyes fall to his loincloth. Whatever he wanted with her, it wouldn't be good. No way would I help him find her, even if he killed me.

"I don't know where Kat is, and even if I did, I wouldn't tell you."

His tail swished behind him in a slightly familiar gesture. *Strange...*

He said nothing, and I kept going, trying to bluff my way out of this. The boulder was hot and hard at my back, reminding me that I was trapped.

"My mate is Gahn Taliok. He'll be back here any minute, so you'd better keep your *fucking* distance."

God, I hoped that wasn't a bluff. I hoped Taliok was alive down there. That he was OK, and that he was in fact coming for me. Although, the idea of him fighting this guy turned my stomach. Taliok was so strong, so fierce and powerful. I knew he'd die to protect me. But if he had to fight this lizard-man, he might actually die. If he hadn't already.

The reptile monster stared at me a moment longer. Then his massive head turned as if he'd been distracted by something. He angled himself towards the edge of the rock we stood on, looking down.

What's down there? What does he see? Taliok? Or more enemies? Maybe even ones that look like him...

Clutching at the rock behind me, I leaned, trying to look down, too. But it was impossible from my position, with the boulder behind me and the scaly wall of the reptile alien's body in front of me.

But I didn't need to see. Because I heard it. The cry of my name shaped by Taliok's raging voice.

He's alive.

The roar of my name could have split the fucking mountain. It echoed everywhere, pounding in my head.

More tears streamed as relief caught in my thick throat. *He's OK. He's OK.*

But if he came up here, would he stay that way? New panic filled me, panic at the idea of Taliok suffering the same fate as the other warrior who'd come up here, his body falling lifeless from the rocks.

But how could I stop it? If Taliok had seen me, or scented me, which he probably had considering I was bleeding, then he'd be on his way up here as fast as humanly possible. Or, er, alienly possible. Which was really fucking fast.

Can I push this guy down? Can I kill him first? I stared at the Godzila-like creature scenarios whirring through my head. But all of them would be impossible. He was more than eight feet of raw reptilian power. And I was five-foot-four of not very impressive human power.

But his next words left me stunned, all my plans halting.

"Your mate returns and you are safe. I will leave you now."

Huh?

Before I could even process that, he stuffed his knife into the strap of his loincloth, then placed the handle of his bloodied spear between his teeth. He crouched, then leapt with insane, raw animal strength, landing on the rock above my head and climbing up and across it with ease, moving like a gecko. If a gecko were eight feet long with scales that looked like armour.

With a flash of his dark, spiked tail, he was gone, disappearing around the rock wall and into the crevice.

I stared after him in half-confused, half-terrified wonder. *He really is gone. Just like that.*

The scrabbling of claws and crackle of falling rocks made me jerk my head back. A huge, bloodied alien hand appeared on the ledge before hoisting up the rest of the giant body attached to it.

That scarred, beautiful, familiar body.

Taliok straightened, standing tall and staring at me. His gaze consumed me.

His chest heaved, his face twisting into a snarl, his expression still warped from battle. He looked more like a beast than I'd ever seen him, almost feral. A brutal creature of the desert. And yet I felt no fear. Not like I had with the other brute a few moments ago. Because this was Taliok.

My Taliok.

My mate.

TALIOK

y scream of Melanie's name shook the air. But it did nothing to call her back to me. She did not answer. And my fear grew. *I did not protect her well enough. If she has been harmed...*

The world would never be the same. Because I would destroy it.

I forced myself to calm enough to inhale deeply, searching for her scent among the heat and the dust and the stones. I found it almost immediately and my chest clenched when I scented the bitter edge to it. *Her blood.*

I wrenched my head and began to run, following the scent. My eyes cast about everywhere, my normally steady diligence dissolving in my panic. *Where is she? She is bleeding. Why is she bleeding? Where is she? Where, where, where?*

Her scent was even stronger when I ended up at the steep incline of the rock face. Surely she had not climbed...

I looked up and saw her. Everything in my world narrowed down to that one, small, human-woman-shaped point. She was standing. She was alive and alert. She was looking upwards and into the crevice. *What does she see up there? A predator, a krixel?* That thought struck yet more fear into my heart. *Why has she gone so high?*

In my haste, I almost didn't register the dead warrior at the bottom of the incline. His chest and neck had been wounded, mortally so. But none of my men were here. So who had done it?

He was crumpled. As if he'd fallen from above.

Certainly, Melanie could not have done it. But then who?

Questions burning, mind racing, I plunged forward, scaling the rocks quickly, muscles bunching, claws grasping. In mere moments, I had reached the ledge where Melanie stood. I pulled myself up, standing, my eyes falling to her small form.

Her face was paler than normal, and her eye shells were gone. From here, she looked unharmed. But there was still that scent, so much stronger now, of her blood.

One breath later, I was before her. My hands brushed her jaw, her scalp under her hood, her neck.

"Where are you injured? What has been done to you?" I heaved, my voice breaking.

"It's nothing. I'm alright. It's just my hands."

She raised the small appendages before me, palms up. Her soft skin was mottled with cuts, blood mixing with the sweat.

It was most certainly not alright! My Melanie had been injured. Her perfect skin had been damaged. But it had not been inflicted by an enemy, I was sure. This was not the work of weapons.

I held her wrists gently, reverently, leaning closer to inspect her wounds. They were not deep.

"Why did you leave the sheltered place? Why did you come all the way up here?"

Her breath shuddered, and I realized she was crying. I raised my head, groaning, moving my hands around her back and drawing her to me.

"I thought I could help you," she cried. "I came up here to push that boulder off if someone was coming."

The boulder?

I looked behind her at the stone she meant. It was large and heavy. I doubted she would have been able to do it.

But the fact that she had tried anyway, tried to help me, was a testament to her warrior's spirit. *She is a true Gahnala, my mate.*

I held her as she shook, sobbing against my chest.

But I am not a true Gahn. I have left her too long. And now she cries her strange human tears.

As I held her, I picked up on another scent. A sharp, bitter one I did not recognize. It was no scent I had ever picked up on, from man, woman, child, or even animal. Immediately, I turned, thrusting Melanie behind my back, keeping her between the boulder she meant to push and me.

"Who was here with you?" I remembered the body at the bottom of the incline. "Who killed the warrior?"

Melanie spoke from behind me as my eyes searched the surrounding area. But other than Galok racing through the valley below me I saw nothing out of the ordinary.

"There was another man. But not a man. Not like you. I'm not sure…"

I spun, gripping her small jaw between my hands.

"Who? What man?" Her words made no sense. *A man, but not a man like you.*

"He was a man in that he could speak to me and he stood on two legs like us," she said. "He had sight stars, but he wasn't of the Sea Sands. He had dark blue skin, and scales, and a mouth like a *crocodile*… or, I guess like an irkdu."

My face got closer and closer to hers as she spoke, as if by getting closer, I could make her words make sense. *Perhaps the heat has gotten to her. Perhaps she has seen something that does not exist.* Because what she described did not exist

But then, who had killed the warrior?

"Whoever he was, he saved me," she continued. "He was terrifying and huge, but he didn't hurt me. Then I thought he was going to stay here and try to hurt you, but he didn't."

I grunted, happy to hear that, but not liking the sound of this irkdu-man-creature Melanie described. My men were currently scouring the mountains for more of Gahn Baldor's men. If he did indeed exist, they would find him.

Whatever Melanie had seen, the scent was already fading. It, or he, was gone, leaving only us. I lowered my forehead to hers, a shock running through me at the feel of her skin against mine.

Words broke out of me.

"I have not felt fear like this in many ages. The fear that I might lose you..."

I did not like the feeling. I felt... Vulnerable. For the first time since I was a child.

Melanie was crying again.

"I know what you mean. I was so scared for you, Taliok. I was so scared you'd be hurt. That's why I came up here. I wanted to do anything I could to help you. I was desperate-"

With a groan, I cut off her words, my mouth crashing to hers. She gasped against me, opening immediately to my tongues, her wetness a sweet balm after the blistering battle. My cock awakened immediately, my body still thrumming from the fight, but I tore myself away. *I cannot go too far now. Her injuries need attending to.*

I swept her up into my arms, cradling her gently but firmly against my chest. Then I began the descent, moving carefully so as not to hurt her further. She curled her injured hands into my chest, letting her head rest against me. Having her so relaxed in my arms, leaning her head on me like that, made me dizzy with joy. I forced myself to keep my wits about me, though. I was not yet convinced we were free from earlier threats.

As I reached the ground, Galok called to me. Kat walked beside him. She seemed totally unharmed, walking with her own strength, shooing Galok's helping hands away. When she saw me carrying Melanie, she started to run, her tiny legs making surprisingly swift progress.

"What happened? What happened to her? Melanie, are you OK?"

Melanie raised her head.

"I'm OK. Shaken up. My hands got cut up. But I'm fine. You?"

Kat moved her head up and down in that distinct human fashion.

"I'm fine."

Galok smiled at her words.

"Gahn Taliok and I have protected you well. You are safe now, Kat."

She looked at him, her expression flat, then walked away, back towards the tents. I followed her, as did Galok, and Melanie let her head roll against me once again.

We picked our way through the crevice back to the plains. By the time the tents came into view, night was falling, casting long shadows. This made me feel both worried and at ease. In the darkness, we could hide better.

But so could our enemies. Including the strange being Melanie had described.

One of my men, Karik, met us on the plains. He raised his tail and then spoke.

"The others are still searching for enemies. So far we have found none. It seemed to be just a small raiding party."

That is what I'd suspected, too. It was good to hear confirmation.

"You have found nothing so far, no other men... Or other strange creatures?" I pressed.

Karik tilted his head, as if unsure what I meant. Even I was unsure what I meant. I hadn't seen whatever Melanie had claimed to see.

"No, Gahn. Nothing. We believe the only ones who came here are now dead. We will keep searching into the night. In the meantime, I brought fresh meat."

"Good," I said. "Build the evening fire."

Karik raised his tail again, then got to work, placing babkit stalks and branches in the pit. Galok went to help him, as did Kat.

"I'm feeling a lot better, now. I can stand on my own," my mate said from within my arms.

I did not want to let her go. Nor did I want to disobey her. I placed her gingerly upon her small feet. She did not wobble. *My strong mate.*

"Come. Let us tend to your hands."

Keeping a protective arm around her back, I led her to one of the other tents. It had been our healers' tent at one point, when the whole tribe had lived here. Now it was mostly used for weapons storage. But I had ordered my healers to leave some supplies for my guards.

In the tent I quickly found and lit a candle, then perused the bone shelves, locating bandages. Below the shelves, I dug with my claws, soon hitting the hard lid of a jar of Lavrika's blood. I pulled it from the ground and then turned to Melanie.

"Please sit. And remove your cloak." I gestured to the ground, and she did so, sighing, letting the fabric fall down around her.

I sat, too, right in front of her, opening the jar. I gazed at her shoulders, her arms. Other than some redness that would probably turn to bruises, she had no other cuts.

"Turn your palms up to me."

She did so, placing her hands in my lap. I ignored the pulse of my cock at her nearness, focusing on her wounds.

After digging in the ground, my claws and hands were filthy. Instead of dipping my fingers into the jar, I dunked the bandages I'd collected. The woven fabric strips dripped as I pulled them out and laid them on Melanie's torn skin. Her breath hissed between her teeth as I did so, and I tensed.

"Does it hurt?"

Her dark eyes moved to mine, then back to her hands.

"A bit. But it already feels better."

Encouraged, I kept going, dipping bandages and then laying them upon her skin. I was no healer, but a minor wound like this would be healed quickly with just Lavrika's blood. Even my paltry skills would be enough. And I was glad. It felt good to take care of Melanie. To make her whole again where she'd been hurt.

When her hands were lined with sopping wet bandages, I stopped my work. I held her forearms gently, unable to stop touching her, running my thumbs along the exquisite softness of her inner wrists. I frowned when I saw the dirt and blood I trailed along her skin. Turning and stretching, I reached for the bone shelves, grabbing a talka stalk. I tore it open, scrubbing the lather between my fingers, under my claws, and up my arms before wiping it away with some unused bandages. Melanie watched me as I did so.

"Can you grab another one of those for me?" she asked. "After the day I've had, I'd love to have a *bath*. And that's the next best thing."

I did as she asked.

"What is a bath? Tell me what it is, and I will find it. And if I cannot find it, I will build it."

She smiled, a beautiful thing, lighting up the darkness.

"It's OK. I don't actually think that would be possible right now. I'll tell you about it another time."

I hoped she would. I wanted to know everything about every one of her desires.

After a few moments, I carefully checked under one of the bandage strips on her palm. The skin was already closed, shiny and pink. I removed the wet woven fabric from her skin. She lifted her palms to her face, shaking her head.

"This stuff is incredible. We really need to find out what it is."

What did she mean, *what it is*? She knew what it was.

"It is Lavrika's blood," I said.

She smiled again.

"I mean, find out what it's made of. The *molecular* structure. Find out how it works."

I stared at her. These were incredible questions. But it made sense, coming from such an incredible creature.

I stood, then helped her to her feet.

"Come. You must eat."

She groaned.

"I have no appetite," she complained as we left the tent and headed for the evening fire, now blazing and strong.

"You will eat," I said, more sternly this time. It felt terrible, unnatural, to give her such a command. To give a command to this small one who already so ruled my heart. But in this, I would not be swayed. She had to eat. She had to stay healthy and strong.

"Fine, fine," she muttered, collapsing onto her rump next to Kat. I sat on her other side, and Karik brought me a bone tray of good fresh meat. Before taking any, I made sure Melanie ate some and took some valok. Thankfully, she did so without further complaint. I watched her small jaw as she chewed, entranced by her loveliness.

Our small group ate in silence. Before long, Kat indicated

she was heading to her own tent, and Galok moved to follow, stationing himself outside it. Karik banked the fire, and I helped Melanie up. I still had the talka stalk she requested, and I handed it to her.

"Thanks," she said. "Let's take this back to your tent."

I tried not to feel such hunger at her words, but I could not stop it. *She is tired and she is healing. She will not want you tonight.* This would be enough. It would have to be enough. Just lying next to her as she slumbered was to be treasured.

Together we entered my tent. There, I lit a candle. I was glad I did so as it allowed me to watch Melanie undress more clearly. She removed her pants and shirt, sitting down in just her skimpy underthings. Underthings I longed to slip my claws beneath.

I sat down across from her as she snapped the talka stalk and squeezed the cleansing gel onto her pink palms. She lathered the stuff, then began to rub it down her neck, closing her eyes and sighing.

I gulped, my throat working, my cock throbbing. Her delicate fingers stroked and smoothed over her perfect skin. It was agony to watch. Erotic beyond belief. But nowhere near enough.

I grabbed up a clean scrap of spare hide from nearby, searching for any excuse to touch her.

"Your hands are still healing," I said thickly. "Let me help you."

She cracked her eyes open, looking from the scrap of hide I held to my face. Then she closed her eyes again and let her head roll back, baring her white throat. The talka gel glistened on her skin.

"Alright," she said softly.

And I, Taliok, Gahn of the mountains, did not need any more encouragement than that.

27

MELANIE

My breathing became shallow as Taliok softly dragged the leather cloth down my throat, wiping the soapy talka stuff away. Goosebumps erupted over my skin. He moved maddeningly slowly, cleaning each inch of my neck, even behind my ears, his breath fanning over my face and making every nerve come to attention.

Now that my hands had been sorted out, all I had left were some bruises and sore spots. After eating, I physically wasn't in too rough shape after today. Mentally was another story, but every moment I spent with Taliok, the fear and the pain of the day lessened. And in its place came the need. Every stroke of Taliok's cloth over my skin made me clench. I felt so fucking empty. And wet.

But I didn't want to move. I didn't want to end this. Not yet. I wanted to bask in the perfection of this moment.

I could hear Taliok's breath coming harder, but his hand remained gentle.

This is turning him on, too.

I opened my eyes, looking down at him. His sight stars

were pulled tight in utter focus as he moved from cleaning my neck to my collarbone, stroking the cloth along to my shoulder. He brushed my hair out of the way with more tenderness than I would have thought possible for a seven-foot-tall alien warrior. But this was Taliok. The most surprising creature I'd ever encountered. In all the best ways. He finished at my shoulder, lifting my arm by the wrist and running the cloth down to my hand with reverent attention, then back up. He repeated it on the other side, then back up again. Then he moved down to my cleavage, his nostrils flaring.

"Take it off," I whispered. Taliok tensed, then moved his claws towards the straps of my bra.

"Wait, I'll do it," I said.

A clueless guy trying to take a girl's bra off was bad enough. It was even worse when he had fatally sharp claws. I only had one bra, after all.

I reached back and unclasped it, tossing it aside, loving the way Taliok's eyes glazed over with desire. He was on his knees between my legs, his cock standing at full attention beneath his loincloth. I closed my eyes again, giving in to the sensations of Taliok running the soft wet leather over my breasts, brushing the nipples, making them tighten. When I moaned softly, Taliok tensed, then kept going.

For a while, he continued in silence. The only sound was our breathing, growing heavier with need. But then, he spoke.

"I liked seeing your wide smile today. I want to see it every day, if possible." He brought the cloth down to my belly button, circling it softly the way he had days ago, when he was helping me onto his mount. His voice rasped. "I want to see joy spill out of you like sunshine. I've never known such light as yours."

Fuck. This was too much. I was going to tell him I loved

him and then jump his damn bones at this rate. And I really, really wanted to actually get clean first. But Taliok's smooth touches were only serving to arouse me.

I took the cloth from him, quickly scrubbing some areas he'd missed, before shimmying out of my panties. When I spread my legs to run the cloth there, Taliok's eyes dropped, darkening with hunger. He watched the drag of my hand through my folds with rapt attention, every muscle tight and bunching under his skin, his huge hands on my splayed knees.

"I smiled because of you," I panted, growing more wet by the second. I was so turned on, so fucking sensitized, that even just running the cloth over myself was a sharp pleasure. Soon, I was done cleaning to my satisfaction, and I tossed the cloth into the pile of my other clothing.

"Taliok," I continued, "part of why I was smiling was because of something I want to tell you."

He wrenched his eyes, with what looked like great effort, away from my pussy, settling on my face.

Here we go.

It was time. I was going to tell him.

There's no going back now.

But I didn't want to go back. Back to the girl with all her walls. The girl who didn't know this kind of love was possible.

I moved up to my knees, pressing gently on Taliok's shoulders, pushing him from his knees into a seated position. I straddled his hips, my fingers quickly undoing his loincloth. His swollen cock sprang free, dark and heavy and fat.

I circled its tip with a finger still slick from the talka gel and he bucked against me. I stared into his eyes as I teased his tip.

"I got interrupted earlier," I said. "But I meant to tell you I'd made a decision. About being your mate."

Taliok stilled. Even his sight stars seemed frozen, no pulsing or tightening or swirling. It was like everything he knew hung in the balance of my next words.

Everything I know, too.

"I love you, Taliok. And I want to be your mate. Your Gahnala."

The words shattered his stillness. His golden sight stars pulsed inward, then exploded, hazing his vision. His hands found their way to my jaw, and he brought my face closer, staring deep into me.

"You speak true, Melanie?"

I nodded in his firm grip, my throat tightening.

"Yes."

His mouth was on mine with no warning, lips searching and opening. I arched against him, my nipples brushing his chest and sending shocks through me. Our tongues brushed, and Taliok's hips snapped against me, the underside of his huge cock jumping against my aching clit. My chest buzzed at the thought of finally taking that cock inside me.

And with that thought in my head, I couldn't fucking wait another second.

I broke our kiss, my hands on his shoulders, adjusting my positioning so that his thick tip was against my slick entrance. I wanted to plunge downward, but it had been a while since anything had been inside me. Anything besides his centre tongue, that was. And that tongue, while impressive, was nothing compared to the circumference of his dick. It was bigger than anything I'd taken, even the huge specialty dildo a client had once sent to me and paid me a pretty penny to use for him on camera.

I went slowly, slipping the tip inside, feeling a mild, pleasurable stretching. I groaned, throwing my head back, and Taliok rocked upward. I pressed back up, too, to stop too much of his hardness from shoving in all at once.

213

"Stay still for a bit," I breathed against him. He took those words as literally as fucking possible. His hands grew into stone vises against my hips. His tail no longer twitched and thrashed behind him. Every muscle was taut and thrumming, but not moving. He barely even breathed, his chest tense and still.

I slipped onto his tip again, this time a little further down, feeling my wetness starting to coat him and ease the way. He was huge. This appendage was definitely in proportion to the rest of him. But so far, there had only been heated pleasure, no pain, Encouraged, I pressed down a little further, then back up, then further down again. Taliok made a desperate, choked sound. But like I had asked him, he didn't move. Even his gaze was pinned on me, not straying even for a moment.

"May I speak?" he groaned, and I laughed softly at his request. *Well, I guess technically speaking is moving, and I told him to stay still.*

"Yes," I answered, needing to hear more of his voice. It vibrated everywhere, resonating in my pussy, making me move down even further onto his hugeness. I had more than half of him inside me, now.

"I have been in many battles," he began. "Killed many men. Killed the krixel as a child and pulled my father's body home. But this, right now, remaining still for *this*," his voice strained on that last word, "has been the greatest challenge in all my warrior's life."

"You can move soon," I murmured, leaning forward and running my hands through his shoulder-length black hair. "So, so soon." It was half a promise and half a demand. I was almost ready. And I would need him to fucking *move*.

Even now, the fullness wasn't enough. It was everything, yet still not enough. I needed the drag of friction moving in and out. I needed the snap of Taliok's hips. The sounds of him coming undone.

He groaned as I sank down, taking him completely.

"When?" He barely got the word out. His eyes rolled back in his head, and I felt every muscle in his legs and pelvis tighten. He was barely keeping himself from driving up into me with everything he had.

I smoothed my hands over his hair again, then across the broad plains of his cheeks in an almost nurturing fashion. Soothing him in his need. When my hands drew near his mouth, his tongues emerged, probing my fingers, sucking them into his mouth. I gasped, my pussy clenching, as he laved my fingers desperately. The feeling of his tongues against my sensitive, newly healed skin was going to drive me over the edge. I began rocking my hips subtly, unable to help myself. I was pretty much accustomed to his size now, and holy shit, did he ever feel good.

"Now, now," I moaned, placing more weight onto my knees on either side of him and lifting my ass, giving him room to move. A shudder ran through his frame, and then he began to pump. He began slowly, as if testing everything, savouring every moment of this new sensation. His cock spears pressed through my folds as he moved, sending shivers of pleasure everywhere. I was already so fucking close to coming, my whole body straining, aching, with the intensity of him inside me. I pressed further forward, my hands moving to grapple against his back.

"Taliok," his name was barely audible, a half-whispered cry.

And with that, my diligent alien warrior totally lost control.

His hips began a merciless rhythm, hard and fast and so fucking good. That speed and intensity almost would have been punishing if we hadn't started off so slow. And if I wasn't so wet for him. I could hear the slick of his cock as he drew back and then drove back in, the sound brutally arousing. Taliok was so quiet, everything bit-down and closed-up with the intensity, his jaw twisting, his tail thrashing. But as his hips began to lose all semblance of rhythm, his movements becoming chaotic and unhinged, sounds began to grit out from between his clenched fangs – the hiss of groaning breath.

"This is too good," he managed to say, sounding hoarse. "I do not deserve such goodness."

The words made my chest ache.

I couldn't think of anyone else who deserved this more. This joy, this pleasure. Heat building deep in my core, I messily pressed my mouth to his, whispering against his lips, "Yes, you do."

His breath sighed out, shaking, against my face, and that sensation hurled me over. I came undone, everything clenching and tightening, my whole body exploding with hot stars of pleasure. Taliok kept thrusting through it, and when I opened my eyes, my pussy pulsing, I saw that his gaze was trained on my face, totally entranced.

"You are... perfect," he said. The words were grunts, His fingers tightened on my hips, and he arched forward and upward, driving into me with one huge, final thrust, spilling everything he had.

Seeing him lose himself to pleasure in my body sent more aftershocks through me. Needily, I leaned forward, teasing his mouth open with my tongue. His mouth devoured mine, and he began more slow soft thrusts. Both of us were so sensitized after coming, but neither of us were ready to stop.

It wasn't long before Taliok's thrusts became harder and faster once again, his breath rough, deep moans escaping his mouth. My hand fell between my legs, strumming my clit as pulsing pleasure built once again. I was going to come, twice in a fucking row, on Taliok's cock.

And it seemed like he was in the same boat. His hips

jerked harder and harder, and I could feel how stiff he was inside me, fat and throbbing. Without warning, he gripped my back and flipped me so that he was on top. As he sank even deeper in this new position, his hips driving forward, he arched and moaned.

Fuck, yes. Me being on top was so fucking good. Having him and all his hugeness over top of me, inside of me, everywhere around me, was absolutely fucking insane. I spread my legs, drawing my knees up and hooking them around his waist. He pressed down against me, one elbow on the ground to keep from crushing me, his free hand running down my throat to my breast. But like before, his eyes were on mine. Ravenous. Demanding and generous at the same time. Devouring and loving.

"I'm going to come again," I moaned, spreading myself even wider for him as he sank into me, over and over again.

"This is... good," Taliok grunted, and I almost wanted to laugh at the typically, serious, Taliok response. But any laughter died in my throat as I came, clutching at his hips, his powerful glutes, feeling his muscles bunch and strain. Taliok's mouth fell to my neck, and the deep groan he let out against my skin moved all the way down my body. He exploded again, both of us pulsing and arching together until we were finally, finally spent.

I didn't think that that spent feeling would last very long, though. If things were always going to be this good, I was going to be begging him to mate every freaking night.

But judging by the way Taliok was staring at me, like I was giving him the world, like I *was* his whole world, I doubted I'd have to beg.

He moved his hips back, slipping out of me, and we both flinched at the sudden loss of connection. Without him, I felt so empty. To overcome the feeling, I pulled him down onto his side next to me and nuzzled in close, my nose to his chest, drinking in his scent. His arms went around me imme-diately, pulling me in tighter. I could feel his nose and mouth brushing the top of my head, breathing into my hair.

And like that, wrapped up in all of Taliok's safety and love, I fell asleep.

28
TALIOK

Melanie fell asleep almost immediately, her perfect body sated. I could not sleep so easily. Though I, too, felt sated, my head was spinning. I was alive with the intensity of life's good joy. The fact that Melanie had created my entire world again, rebuilt it into something new.

When I finally did sleep, it was wrapped in her scent.

I awoke at dawn, the ghost of pale light entering the tent from the gaps. Still half-slumbering, I reached for Melanie, clutching for her, scared that she was gone in my half-sleep, that she was not real. But she was there, her soft back against my chest. She moaned sleepily, easing further back against me, shifting down and pressing her rump against my cock. I hardened immediately, fully awake now, and urged my tip between the tops of her thighs, beginning to thrust, liquid heat unfurling in my pelvis. She moaned again, more loudly, then angled her hips so that my tip met her entrance.

"Slow," she whispered in the half-light. *Slow.* It was so difficult when pure desire slammed through me. But I would never hurt her. I nudged inward, feeling her gasp more than I heard it. She rocked back further, pressing. My hand slipped up her front to the heavy softness of her breast, gripping it. Her nipple became a taut pebble under my palm. It made my cock throb.

"More," my mate breathed, turning her head back to look at me. Unable to refuse her request, unable to refuse her anything, I pressed further, further, until I was fully seated in her, tight heat wrapping my cock.

I buried my face against the top of her head, in her dark hair, curling down around her as I thrusted.

"Taliok," she breathed, and my name in her mouth made me arch. She was saying *my* name. She wanted *me*. Had chosen *me*. Loved *me*.

She is mine.

And I was hers.

Forever hers. Nothing but hers. Nothing without her, but everything with her.

Everything when inside her.

I gripped her breast harder, shuddering as her cunt milked me. At her needy panting, I moved my fingers down to her nub, her *clit*. I circled that small bit of flesh, fascinated by the way she tightened around me. She tightened even harder a moment later, her voice exploding from her throat, breaking with the stiffness of sleep. Three more brutal thrusts and I was exploding, too, filling her completely.

We laid like that for a long time as the light grew stronger outside the tent. Eventually, Melanie wriggled out of my embrace, pulling her slickness away from my cock and making me tense. I watched her as she grabbed up the talka stalk from last night, squeezing some of the remaining gel onto a nearby scrap of hide.

"Good thing we still have some of this," she said. "You've made me all sweaty. Not to mention…"

She looked down as a pulse of seed dripped out of her.

My eyes narrowed, my throat bobbing at the sight. My seed dripping out of my mate's cunt... It was too much. My cock was already stirring again, and I gripped it, grunting. Melanie cleaned herself quickly, and I did the same, though I loathed to remove any trace of Melanie from my skin. I comforted myself with the fact that anything cleaned away would be replaced. I would wet my cock with her every night from here on out if she would have me. And as her heated gaze continually flicked to mine while she readied herself and dressed, it did in fact seem that she would have me.

The sun rising higher behind my mountains, we emerged from the tent. Galok was outside, chewing some meat.

"Kat still sleeps," he said. "Your men are out patrolling, but they have found no more enemies."

I jerked my tail in acknowledgement of what he'd said, frowning. In all my pleasures, it had been easy to forget about what had happened yesterday. But the memory was coming back full force. It was no longer safe to keep Melanie and Kat here. As much as I hated to admit it, it would actually be safer for us at the Cliffs of Uruzai, even with Gahn Fallo there. There, we had much greater numbers.

I will have to send back more men to help guard and patrol here, I thought, already calculating men and numbers in my head. But then Melanie brushed against my elbow, smiling up at me, and I softened. These thoughts of command could wait a little longer.

Nearby, Kat emerged from her tent, yawning loudly and scrubbing her hand over her shorn head before pulling up her hood.

"Morning," she croaked. Galok handed her some meat he'd already prepared, and valok. For once, she took it from him without arguing. I fetched some meat and valok for Melanie, too, and spoke to her as she munched contentedly away.

"We will prepare to return to the Cliffs of Uruzai today."

Kat frowned, kicking a pebble. "Aw, man. For real? It's so cool here. We were just getting started."

"It is not safe. Not with Gahn Baldor's men potentially launching another attack." And it wasn't just Gahn Baldor's men I was worried about, now. But also the apparition Melanie had described. The man who looked like an irkdu…

"He's right," Melanie said from beside me, and her belief in my decisions made pride surge. "We got lots of samples to bring back. That will be enough for now. We can always reassess later and come back if it's safe."

My pride pulsed stronger. My mate, my Gahnala, was wise indeed.

"That reminds me," Melanie said, this time just to me. "In all the chaos we left our stuff from yesterday behind. Can we go get it?"

"Yes," I told her.

I, too, had left something behind in the valley that I needed to retrieve.

Something precious.

MELANIE

After eating, Taliok and I made our way back over the boulders and rocks to get to the valley while Kat stayed behind to pack up with Galok. In the deep, shadowy crevice between the mountain walls, evidence of the battle was mostly gone. The bodies had been carried away, I assumed, by Taliok's men. Here and there I saw dark dashes of dried black blood on red stone, and my insides twisted. The thought that Taliok could have died, yesterday... That he could have died without us ever getting together was a terrifying one. I revelled in the feeling of his huge, sturdy hand gripping my arm to keep me steady. He was so solid. So dependable and real and alive. And I was so fucking lucky.

Once in the valley, we worked quickly. It didn't take long to recover the samples Kat and I had organized yesterday, and I tucked them into my pack. I turned to leave but Taliok swished his tail.

"There is something, I, too, must retrieve."

What does he need to get? Did he leave a weapon behind or something?

He led me a little ways down the valley. As we walked, my

eyes cast upwards, up to the ledge I'd been on yesterday. A shiver ran through me when I remembered that visceral fear. The fear first of the enemy warrior, and then of that completely unknown alien, the huge reptile. Although, even though he'd scared the living daylights out of me, I hoped he was OK out there somewhere. He hadn't hurt me, and he hadn't purposely tried to scare me. He'd actually helped me, in his own way, by killing that other warrior. He'd seemed… weirdly… kind? His words echoed in my head, "You are safe now." But then other words echoed, "Tell me where to find the other female," and my thoughts of his kindness disappeared. I didn't wish him harm, but I also hoped he wasn't out there looking for a human girl to scoop up into his scaly arms.

Taliok stopped and crouched, and I shook thoughts of the reptile man away, focusing instead on the man before me. Taliok stood, then turned, his clawed hands full of stones. My breath caught in my throat.

Of course.

All the beautiful stones he'd collected for my Gahnala-Kai Rek.

"Now that we are mated, and you have agreed to become my Gahnala, I could not leave them. I had already spent too long fantasizing about seeing them against your skin," he said. My ribs expanded with what felt like light. I felt weightless and floaty, like I could lift right off the ground.

"You know, in moments like this, human men get down on one knee where I'm from."

Taliok cocked his head in confusion, but did so anyway, moving to one knee. He looked like a Greek statue on steroids, a carved testament to muscle and masculinity and brutal alien beauty. Seeing him down on one knee, his huge hands filled with precious stones he'd collected just for me, made my throat swell. Tears spilled out of my eyes, and since I'd lost my sunglasses yesterday, I couldn't hide them.

Alarmed, Taliok moved to rise, but I shook my head, rubbing my eyes.

"No, no. It's OK. Stay there. You're perfect."

He watched me as if unsure, then grunted.

"It is you who is perfect. Perfect and strange and wondrous."

Laughing tearfully, I moved down to my knees, too, shuffling up to him. I cupped his broad, scarred face in my hands.

"I love you," I said. Taliok's sight stars pulsed, his brow contracting. He opened his fanged mouth to reply, but he didn't need to. I already felt his love, every moment. He made me feel it. Made me believe it.

I pressed upwards, cutting off his words with a kiss. He met my mouth eagerly, lips and tongues pressing and swiping. My hands slipped down his neck, down his chest and arms to his hands. While kissing him, I closed his long fingers into fists around the shining stones, then placed my hands on top.

A moment later, still holding his hands, I broke off the kiss. I could have stayed in those mountains, Taliok's mountains, kissing him forever, but it was time. Time to get back to Kat and Galok and the rest of the tribes at the Cliffs of Uruzai.

Time to begin our new life.

OTHER BOOKS BY URSA DAX

Fated Mates of the Sea Sand Warlords

Alien Tyrant

Alien Enemy

Alien Orphan

Alien Reject

Alien Exile

Alien Hunter

Alien Victor

Alien Shield

Alien Keeper

Alien Claw

Alien Heart

Alien Mask

Alien Storm

Alien Hope

Brides of the Stone Sky Gods

Alien God

Berserker God

Holiday Romances of Elora Station

Chimera for Christmas

Alien Orc for Christmas